The Heirs of the
MEDALLION
BOOK FOUR

TUKOR

David Sage

With Thanks

To the ladies at the library in Cody, Wyoming who encouraged me to come and do a book signing, then asked me back to give a talk on historical fiction. To Katie, Ann, Mallory, and Katie B. who invited me to share creative writing with their 7th Grade students at Sheridan Junior High. To Vicki, Jennifer, Dylan, Robin and the PTO of Story School, who allow me to tell stories twice a month. Thank you all for making me a part of your activities.

To 'Yoder,' for your wisdom about the art of writing...I can never fully express my appreciation. To my son Ty, for your counsel on the publishing world... thank you for being such a steadying influence.

To Dave and Beth for your enthusiasm, to my wife Marcia for awesome proofing and daughter Tierney for priceless editing…each of you is a part of this book!

David Sage
Story, Wyoming

Table of Contents

Foreword

IN MID-JUNE OF 1997, Juan and Sophia Valdez, 12 year-old twins from Center, Colorado, were given three unusual items by their great-grandfather. The first was a five-foot long Incan sling. The second was a cloth shirt of almost impenetrable Incan armor. The third was an ancient silver medallion from the Incan Empire, the surface of which is engraved with strange markings.

The use of the sling and armor has been a family tradition for 500 years. The medallion, passed down from generation to generation, holds a great secret, which the family will one day discover. Great Grandfather instructs them to look through the square hole in the medallion at the rising sun on the Summer Solstice. When they do, the twins view a skirmish between Incan warriors and conquistadors. Great Grandfather then begins the epic tale of the family's history with the medallion, which began with that battle.

The first book in the series, ***Adzul,*** recounts the story of a young warrior's flight through the Andes to save the medallion. Pursued by conquistadors, he is nearly killed several times before making his way through Central America months later. Just when he thinks he's safe, he encounters other conquistadors bent on pillaging the Aztec Empire.

The second book, ***Cuto,*** chronicles the story of Adzul's grandson, who leaves his village to seek adventure in new town of Santa Fe far to the north. Befriended by Pueblo Indians, Cuto and his companions are forced into hiding when a sadistic soldier determines to slay him.

Lita picks up the narrative more than 60 years later. She and her brother Rutu set out to find the Great Water in the northwest, talked about by traders bringing ivory carvings to trade with the Pueblo Indians. Brutal winter conditions stop them in the far north. To avoid starvation, they join Crow Indian friends in a desperate hunt for The Beast.

Book four, ***Tukor,*** is the story of Lita's great, great grandson continuing her quest more than a century later.

Family Wearers of the Medallion	Friends of the Family
Qist Incan warrior (Circa 1540) |	
Adzul Son of Qist, married Itta (Aztec) (Circa 1540–1612) |	*Quauhtli,* Itta's brother *Yaoti,* warrior
Cuto Grandson of Adzul, married Ria (Circa 1590–1680) |	*Feather,* Pueblo chief *Swallow,* Feather's daughter *Walks in the Grass,* warrior *Backward Looking,* warrior
Lita Granddaughter of Cuto, sister of Rutu (Circa 1650–1740) |	*Badger Snarling,* Ute warrior *Knows No Fear,* Crow chief *Chattering Squirrel,* Crow boy – renamed *Beast Blinder*
Ria II Granddaughter of Lita, married Sand, the great, great grandson of Swallow (Circa 1710–1805) |	
Tukor Grandson of Ria II (Circa 1785–1895)	

CHAPTER 1
Disaster

THE PIECE OF SILVER had chilled so rapidly in the -25 temperature it was hurting Juan's fingers. Overhead, millions of brilliant stars were rapidly disappearing as the sky brightened in the east behind the jagged peaks of the Sangre de Cristo Mountains.

He hastily donned a pair of Thinsulate gloves from the pocket of his snowmobile suit and turned to his twin sister.

"Why do we always come out so early? We've got at least 10 minutes before the sun clears the peaks. It's insane with this cold! All we have to do is step back into the house and stay warm." He stomped his insulated boots on the snow and gestured at the home 30 feet behind them, but neither of them made a move to go inside.

"You'd think we'd know better now," laughed Sophia, her voice slightly muffled by the wool balaclava covering her head and face. Her black eyes twinkled through the opening in the garment. "The sun has to be above the mountains before the medallion reveals anything…if it's going to."

"It hasn't failed for the last three solstices," answered Juan, pulling his fleece neck-warmer up over chin and nose against the biting cold. "And I don't think it's going to fail us now." He stared at the circular piece of metal in his hand. Odd marks were cut in its surface around the square hole in the middle. "I wonder what these markings are. Even Great Grandfather has no idea."

"I think they're tied to the medallion's secret," answered Sophia thoughtfully. "I don't know how a piece of silver can have a secret, but that's what Qist told Adzul 500 years ago when he passed the medallion on with instructions that it must not fall into the hands of the conquistadors. I'll bet that every ancestor of ours since then has wondered about the instructions, particularly those that wore it."

"It's interesting, because while the wearers have protected the medallion, it's protected them as well. Including us, I might add," said Juan. "It's saved our lives three times since we got it. It saved us from the cougar attack the first autumn after Great Grandfather passed it down to us, from the avalanche last winter, from the the deadfall in the Gunnison River last summer! Not to mention a couple of other incidents."

"I've a feeling we're going to learn more about the secret," she observed. "Great Grandfather knows of no one in the history of the family who's been able to see into the past the way we have. And both of us have done it, even though you are the wearer."

"Only because I'm a minute or so older," remarked Juan. He hunched his shoulders against the cold and stared at the mountains. "Looking through the medallion at the Summer Solstice is fine, but these winter mornings are brutal," he added. "Finally," he exclaimed with relief, "the sun's climbing above the peaks."

In spite of themselves, both feared nothing would happen when they peered through the medallion at the sun. Juan held up the silver piece and, heads pressed together, they stared at the bright orb through its square hole. The instant it rose above the last peak, black smoke rolled across the opening, they breathed a sigh of relief, and then held their breath in anticipation. Although the scene around them remained unchanged, it was as though they were looking at a tiny movie screen.

Gradually the smoke drifted away...to be replaced by rolling gray water stretching endlessly away under a clouded sky. Swells rose and fell, bits of white foam blowing off the tops. Then a dark object intruded from the right. It was the prow of a boat. Shortly, the whole craft was visible: about 20 feet long and made of dark wood. Four men on each side were wielding long paddles furiously, a man behind them in the stern steering with a sweep. A tenth man stood in the bow clasping what looked like a long pole. Suddenly, on the far side of the boat there was a disturbance in the water and a dark shape, far longer than the boat, rose and sent a great blast of water and spray up into the air. Excited voices could clearly be heard as the men stopped paddling and stared at the glistening form not 15 feet away.

The man in the bow raised the pole in one hand and hurled it with great force at the huge shape. From the front of the pole protruded a white barbed point 18 inches long. The kids realized the pole was a harpoon. The instant it struck, the man flung one hand up and the paddlers began to pull back as hard as they could. But before they gained any distance, an enormous two-sided tail lifted high out of the water and slammed down on the surface with a huge splash. The end of the tail closest to the boat brushed the front gunwale, splitting the wood and driving the bow straight down; the stern shot up like a catapult and the men were thrown through the air like a handful of pebbles. In the next instant it was over; once again undisturbed gray swells rolled on toward the distant horizon. Abruptly the scene disappeared, and the morning sun shone through the medallion...

CHAPTER 2

Beginnings

IN STUNNED SILENCE Juan and Sophia stared at each other oblivious to the cold.

"No one could have survived that!" muttered Juan. "Did you see the heavy clothing those men were wearing? Everyone except the harpooner had mittens; it must have been really cold. They would have sunk like rocks!"

"They were hunting a whale, but that boat didn't look very maneuverable. It seemed heavy and awkward, like it was carved from a tree trunk," exclaimed Sophia. "It certainly wasn't as flimsy as a canoe, and much bigger, but just a touch of that fluke split the hull."

"A 'touch' may be an understatement," said her brother, "the power of those animals is unbelievable!" He shook his head in amazement.

"You're right about the clothes though," observed Sophia. "There wasn't a head in sight when the scene disappeared. How could anyone have survived?"

"Great Grandfather's the only one person who knows the answer to that question," replied Juan. "Let's get breakfast for Mrs. Martinez; we can be at his house by 8:00." He slipped the thong around his neck and tucked the piece of silver under his shirt, gasping as the cold surface touched his skin. They hurried to the home of the widow who had been married to one of their great grandfather's oldest friends. She was in her 90's and had started to go blind, along with becoming forgetful. The family, scared she would leave the stove on and burn the house down, had been ready to place her in the retirement home in Alamosa when the twins stepped in. Fearful she would just waste away in the unfamiliar surroundings, they had designed a schedule to prepare meals for her each day. Juan made breakfast before leaving for school and Sophia cooked supper when she got home.

An hour later the two were knocking on the door of the small white house where Great Grandfather lived. The beautiful handmade rocking chair, porch furniture, and flower pots of summer had long since been put away, and the stained decking under its sloping roof was swept clean of snow. The polished oak door opened almost immediately, as though their relative had been waiting behind it for them.

"I've been up since before dawn, wondering what you would see," said Great Grandfather with a smile, beckoning them inside. Of modest height and slender, he was dressed in a wool shirt and jeans, with stocking feet thrust into a pair of old well-worn leather sandals. His brown face was framed with pure white hair; bright black eyes stared over a slightly aquiline nose and strong chin. He looked to be in his 70's but was actually almost 102. Renowned as a gardener throughout the San Luis Valley, Great Grandfather did a brisk summer business out of a large vegetable garden behind the house; in the winter he called on old friends throughout the Valley and attended all of Juan's and Sophia's athletic events. Sundays during the fall he was riveted to the TV when the Denver Broncos played.

After nearly nine decades of wearing the medallion, he had passed it on to the twins 18 months earlier, as the youngest members of the family. This was in accordance with the directive of their ancestor Qist, 500 years earlier, when he ordered his son Adzul to flee the Incan Empire with the strange piece of silver. He and his descendants were to wear and protect the medallion until its great secret was revealed.

Great Grandfather had also passed on to Juan and Sophia two ancient Incan skills: the use of the

deadly sling and the woven pattern of their incred-
ibly strong cloth armor. For centuries, members of
the family had passed down both talents. The armor
shirts were donned for dangerous occasions, but the
slings were always carried, wrapped around the waist
under clothing.

Also in accordance with the ancient directive,
every wearer had dutifully observed the rising sun
through the square hole of the medallion at the summer and winter solstices but, until the summer of 1993,
nothing unusual had ever occurred. When the twins
first raised the ornament that year, they'd witnessed
the sights and sounds of an ancient battle. Each suc-
ceeding Solstice had revealed an incident in the family's
history with the medallion and Great Grandfather
had filled in the circumstances of that era. Now, he
listened intently as they described what they'd seen.
At the end, he stared for a long time into his coffee
cup, deep in thought.

"Tukor," he finally said in a soft voice, "he and
his wolf." The twins waited expectantly, knowing not
to interrupt the old man when his thoughts roamed
deep in the past.

CHAPTER 3

Starving

The rocky hillside was baking in the morning sun. A lizard flitted across the sandy soil to perch on a small boulder, its skin changing color to blend with the tan, irregular surface. High in the cloudless sky, the only motion was that of a vulture making lazy circles as it sought some morsel of carrion on the desert floor; nothing else stirred.

In the slight shadow of a giant saguaro cactus, 50 yards from the hill, a pair of black eyes searched the slope for any sign of movement. They belonged to a 12-year-old boy lying motionless on the ground. His shoulder-length black hair was held in place by a red headband; the long white cotton shirt and matching knee length pants were bound with a colorful cloth belt. Knee-high leather moccasins completed his garb.

Hours before, in the dark, he'd climbed up a narrow shaft to the desert floor from a cave in a remote box canyon 200 feet below. Footholds cut in the rock by the Ancient Ones ages before had converted the shaft to an escape route against enemies gaining access to the canyon. In peaceful times, it afforded access to the desert floor for hunting.

It was on such an expedition for jackrabbits, a few days earlier, that the boy had come upon the dead body of a wolf. The burned bushes around it, and its scorched hair, suggested the cause of death was a lightning strike during a fierce storm the day before. The wolf's swollen udders revealed it was a nursing female and the boy had spent the intervening days unsuccessfully looking for her litter. He'd covered the ground in an ever-widening circle from the body but had found no trace of a lair. Time was running short because the pups couldn't survive much longer without food. The hillside in front of him was almost half a mile from where he'd found her, but had enough rocks and boulders to screen a den. It was his last chance; any living pups would certainly be dead by morning.

His eyes snapped to the left. Was that a flicker of motion in the shadow of two small boulders tipped against each other? There it was again! Out of the shadow staggered a tiny black form to sit and tip its head back. It was clearly making a noise but the distance was too great for the boy to hear it. Suddenly it collapsed on its side and lay still. Throwing caution to the winds, the boy leaped to his feet and sprinted toward the boulders. When he arrived, the pup didn't even raise its head and he thought it had died. A minute later, however, as he held it in cupped hands, its eyes fluttered open.

"Don't die, little one," whispered the boy. "I'm going to take care of you." Holding the pup carefully, the boy ran across the desert to the nondescript pile of rocks that disguised the chimney opening. As he carefully placed the little black body inside his shirt for the descent, its eyes briefly opened again and stared at him as though telling him to hurry. Carefully placing fingers and toes in the correct starting handholds (failure to do so would leave him hopelessly contorted halfway down by the Ancients' crafty design), the youth sped down the shaft until the sky was a small light above and a rushing underground stream below loud in his ears.

Slipping through the narrow passage beside the stream, he entered the back of a long cave with walls covered by paintings, and raced toward the circle of sunlight marking its opening. Outside, he burst through the screen of bushes hiding the cave and whistled for his horse. A bay filly grazing in lush grass under the cottonwoods raised her head and nickered. In a minute they were racing down the valley toward a cluster of small white houses 1,000 yards away.

"Mother, mother, do we have any goat's milk?" shouted the lad as he leaped from the horse, one hand protectively covering the little bundle in his shirt.

"The crock in the stream has some," answered his mother from the enormous vegetable garden behind the houses where she and other women were picking squash. In minutes the boy was dribbling milk from a finger into the tiny mouth.

"Thus began the bond of Tukor and the wolf he called Shadow," said Great Grandfather, leaning back in his chair. "It was a friendship destined to continue for many years."

CHAPTER 4

Popé Rebellion

"WHO WAS TUKOR AND when did this happen?" asked Sophia.

"He was Lita's great, great grandson," replied the old man. "He rescued the whelp in the late 1790's and received the medallion from his 95 year-old grandmother Ria II six years later."

"I've noticed something," interjected Sophia. "Everyone you've told us about who's worn the medallion, Adzul, Cuto, and Lita, has lived to be very old. You yourself are 102! Not only that, but each has been remarkably strong and active in old age. Adzul hit three quail in a row with headshots from his sling at almost 100 (and made sure Cuto heard about it!).

We know Cuto was going strong at 80, and now you say Lita's granddaughter lived to be 95! It must be the medallion." She stared at her relative.

"Perhaps so," replied the old man. "We've all experienced some of the medallion's mysterious properties and longevity seems to be part of its power. You mentioned Cuto going strong at 80. Well, late in his 90's, he and his sling were instrumental in the great Santa Fe uprising against the Spanish!"

"If we hadn't seen you, at your age, bury a stone in a tree with your sling, that would be hard to believe," said Juan, nodding his head at the memory. "How did Cuto get involved in a fight when he was that old?" His relative grinned.

"Well, you'll remember that Cuto had many conflicts with the conquistadors: he nearly died from the whipping by Lieutenant Marquez, was attacked at the pueblo along with the Indians, and finally was set upon in his own home canyon. He had his victories, but vindication finally came in the Popé Uprising of 1680, nine years after Lita, Rutu, and Beast Blinder came home.

"It all started during the 1670's, when a drought hit the Santa Fe region, causing great hardship for both Indians and the Spanish. Streams dried up, crops died, and people everywhere suffered severe food shortages. The Apache, taking advantage of the weakened Pueblo

Indians, increased their raids against the pueblos and the Spaniards as well.

"All of this combined to fan the flames of unrest against the conquistadors. For more than 60 years they had ruled with a cruel, iron hand, in some cases practically enslaving the Indians, and the resentment in surrounding pueblos had long been smoldering. Unfortunately, not all the friars were as kind as Father Montoya had been and, after his return to Spain, Feather's pueblo came under increasing harassment by the new "men in black" for their ritual practices. In 1675, the Governor ordered nearly 50 Indian medicine men arrested and imprisoned; three were executed and a fourth committed suicide before they could hang him. At this, the pueblos began to amass forces around Santa Fe and demanded the Governor release the rest of the men. Fearing attack, he released the captives. One of them was a man named Pópay, or Popé, from the Ohkay Owingeh Pueblo." Great grandfather leaned back and stared at the twins.

"The story of our family's involvement in the Popé rebellion took place many decades before Tukor was born. Are you sure you want to hear about it?"

"Every word!" exclaimed the twins almost in unison.

"Very well, we'll digress and backtrack next Saturday," said the old man, drinking the last of his coffee, a twinkle in his eye. The twins looked at each other askance. They knew better than to ask him to go on; he was fond of leaving them with a cliffhanger!

"Bear in mind," Great Grandfather began the following week, "The Popé rebellion came several years after Cuto's grandkids Lita and Rutu returned from Crow country with Beast Blinder. But, the family's involvement had its roots decades earlier when Cuto and Ria saved the ten-year-old Pueblo girl Swallow from certain death after a savage beating at the hands of a Comanche warrior. This act cemented a relationship with the Pueblo leader Feather (her father) that lasted for generations. Later, as a teenager, Swallow was captured by Apache horse raiders. Feather and Cuto mounted a rescue and Cuto used an ancient Incan technique to terrorize the Apache camp. This history forms the background for Cuto's ability to persuade Pueblo warriors to fight in the Popé Rebellion." His eyes closed as he visualized the events.

CHAPTER 5

Fear

Two horsemen approached the small settlement of white houses clustered on the floor of an enormous desert canyon. Shadows were creeping out from the great rock walls to the west and the face of the eastern cliffs was radiant orange in the setting sun. The riders had come upstream ten miles, from a break in the sheer escarpment that allowed access down into the canyon. As they approached, people working in numerous vegetable gardens waved greetings. They waved back, glancing at the vast horse herd grazing up-canyon, before turning left toward what appeared to be the perpendicular western wall of the canyon. Only when they drew close did a great lateral split in the cliff become visible. It extended 200 feet to the cliff top and formed a narrow passageway angling into the rock to the left. The corridor was 25 feet wide and a stream flowed out of it to join the creek near the village.

Just inside the crack a six-foot rock wall had been built across the passage. In the middle of the wall was a heavy wooden gate just wide enough for one horse to pass through at a time. A man stationed at the gate opened it for the horsemen. Two similar obstructions were encountered in the dimly lit pathway before the riders emerged into a beautiful box canyon. Several clusters of horses fed on lush grass covering its floor and tall cottonwoods shaped the course of the creek flowing from its far end, more than half a mile away. Close at hand were three small white houses with extensive vegetable gardens behind them and colorful flower beds decorating front and sides.

"What news from the pueblo?" called a white-haired man sitting on a stump sharpening a knife with a bit of flint.

"Snorts Like A Bull says the attack is planned during the next moon, when the summer is hottest," replied Rutu, slipping from his horse. Now almost 30, the Aztec warrior's slender body belied great strength. His younger companion, whose brown face was clearly that of an Indian, grabbed the reins of both animals.

"I'll rub them down and turn them loose," said Beast Blinder. Rutu nodded his thanks and squatted beside the knife sharpener.

"Many of the pueblos are committed to Popé but not all, Grandfather. Even though the Spanish soldiers are few in Santa Fe, the people still fear their guns. When the time comes, it's not certain how many will actually fight," explained Rutu. "Snorts Like A Bull is fearless, as was his grandfather, but some of the warriors are hesitant."

"And Swallow? What does she say?" asked Cuto with a frown.

"She stands with her grandson. But she did ask if you would come and talk with the fighters. The conquistadors have been cruel for so long that some of them are intimidated. These men have heard of your exploits with Feather and she thinks your words would encourage them." Before the old man could answer they were hailed by a cheerful voice. Approaching them at a gentle walk was a pinto bearing a beautiful young woman, long black hair held in place by a blue headband, a pretty two-year-old girl perched in front of her on the horse. The little one was waving both arms in greeting.

"Look who's home. It's Uncle Rutu and Beast Blinder!" exclaimed Lita with a big smile. She swung the girl down into the arms of the waiting Indian who immediately began tickling her belly, eliciting shrieks of laughter.

Sliding from the horse, Lita slipped off its headgear and with a gentle slap on the rump sent it toward the tall grasses nearby. Hanging the bridle on a peg in the side of the house, she joined her brother and grandfather.

"How's Swallow?" she asked.

"Spry as ever," replied Rutu. "She noticed the little white filly, the last time she was here. Wants to trade Grandmother two sets of beaded moccasins for her!"

"I bet she's thinking about her grandson's new baby daughter," laughed Lita. "Grandmother will probably drive a hard bargain for that horse!" Everyone chuckled because Ria and Swallow, both close to 90, were like sisters except when it came to the matter of horse-trading.

Cuto and Ria had saved Swallow from death, on their way to Santa Fe, decades before. She was devoted to them and had spent many years riding and training horses in the secret canyon. Both women had a gift with horses and still rode, although they left the training to younger members of their respective families. But occasionally a horse in the Pueblo herd would catch Ria's eye, or one of the Aztec animals would appeal to Swallow. The negotiations that followed were a source of great amusement to the families!

"Snorts Like A Bull says the pueblos will rise against the conquistadors within 30 days," said Rutu, changing the subject. "He wants Grandfather to talk to the warriors. Some fear the guns, even though the Spanish will be greatly outnumbered."

"Perhaps we can do something to allay their fears," said Cuto mysteriously.

CHAPTER 6

Descendants

GREAT GRANDFATHER PAUSED to take a bite of his doughnut. It was Saturday morning and he'd made glazed doughnuts as a special treat for the twins. Normally they'd have opted for some fruit to go with the hot chocolate, because of sports activities in the afternoon, but this was Christmas vacation and they had a few days off.

"Snorts Like A Bull was Swallow's grandson?" asked Sophia. She'd been curious about the life of the Pueblo girl.

"Yes. After Cuto and Feather rescued her from the Apache the second time she was taken from the pueblo, she developed into such an accomplished rider and trainer the warriors were a bit scared by her. Furthermore, in those years, she really preferred working with Ria to living at the pueblo so she wasn't around the young men very often. When Feather finally built a sufficient horse herd to mount all his warriors, she moved home to train them. One day an Indian named Traps A Wolf showed up from a pueblo near what is now Taos, wanting to learn horsemanship. Swallow was 23 and strikingly beautiful." Sophia's eyes sparkled at the idea of romance. The old man noticed and deliberately paused to take another bite of his doughnut.

"Every day Traps A Wolf appeared the minute she left the pueblo. In the beginning he had a thousand questions about horses, but when she caught him repeating the same ones (just to hear her talk), he switched to needing long, long riding lessons—claiming he just couldn't get it right, although she knew he was becoming an expert. Swallow was smitten as well and her other students didn't get much time with her! Finally, he proposed during a ride in the hills just as the edge of the setting sun lit the horizon ablaze in brilliant orange. Traps A Wolf had become very popular at the pueblo and after they were married he never went home. They had four children. Unfortunately, the three oldest and their father died from the coughing disease that struck some years later. The youngest, Haze, grew up to be a great leader in the battles against Apache raiders. Snorts Like A Bull was his son."

"And Lita? She had a two-year-old by now it seems," said Sophia.

"Yes, a year or two after the big trip, she traded three horses to a young man from far to the south who had fled from oppressive conquerors. He talked about great mountains and bitter winters, sparking memories in Cuto of Adzul's stories. Months later, he returned: he'd gone back to rescue his family but they were dead and the village destroyed. His horses were strong and healthy, despite the enormous distance he'd traveled. Seeing his love for horses, Lita encouraged him to stay and become a trainer. A year later they were married and had a little girl they named Chickadee." Sophia nodded and smiled her approval.

"You mentioned a drought after Lita and Rutu got home," said Juan. "How did those in the canyon survive?"

"It was amazing," replied Great Grandfather. "For all those years, indeed for centuries the two creeks never dried up! They must have been supplied by a deep underground aquifer; the water was channeled into a wonderful system of irrigation ditches which kept gardens and grasslands flourishing in the canyons. Both people and horses thrived the entire time, although there was an additional contributing factor," he added mysteriously.

"What was that?" Juan wanted to know. Dark eyes twinkled in the old brown face.

"Why, after Swallow was rescued in the fireball raid, no one ever attacked the canyon again! No matter how often the Apache and Comanche raided Santa Fe, or the pueblos, they rarely ventured into the canyon and then only to trade. There were whispers in their councils that demons guarded the Aztecs and their horses…"

"The man-beast," murmured Sophia.

CHAPTER 7
Legends

Cᴜᴛᴏ ꜱᴀᴛ ɪɴ ᴛʜᴇ ʟᴀʀɢᴇ underground kiva, flanked by his son Necalli on the right and his grandson Rutu on the left. Beside Rutu sat Beast Blinder. A small fire burned on the floor and the circular room was filled with warriors. Snorts Like A Bull sat facing him across the fire.

"Many years ago, long before most of you were born," began the Aztec, "when Swallow was a girl, the Apache captured her and the horses she was bringing to this pueblo." There were grunts of acknowledgement from the older men present.

"Chief Feather had lost his daughter once before, to a Comanche war party. He was not going to lose her again. He picked four warriors and we tracked the raiders to a remote valley in the mountains far to the south." Again there were grunts of agreement because the story had become legendary among the people. The details of the fight itself, however, were hazy because none of the five Pueblo warriors had actually been in the Apache camp when it started. Cuto now used this to his advantage.

"Strange things happened that night. It's told in the Apache camps that fire and death walked among those warriors. They fled for their lives, only to encounter the arrows of the Pueblo! Few survived!" Murmurs of awe and respect for the old Aztec rippled through the audience. Grateful though they were for his friendship, the stories endowed him with an almost mystical persona. Some said the piece of silver worn around his neck made him invincible against any enemy.

"The conquistadors have been cruel to your people and mine," Cuto went on. "In fact, one of them almost whipped me to death." Rising, he slowly lifted his white shirt to expose his back. In the flickering light, a great mass of scars crisscrossing the skin was clearly visible. Grunts of anger rose from the audience. Lowering the shirt, he resumed his seat.

"The leader Popé has called for an uprising against the invaders during the coming moon," he said slowly. "Let it be known that I and my family will stand with you to drive them out." There was a long silence as the implications of the statement sank in. Snorts Like A Bull finally leaned forward, eyes intense.

"It is an honor to have the great warrior and friend of my grandfather join us. Every man in the pueblo will fight beside you!" he declared. A loud chorus of affirming shouts sounded throughout the kiva.

CHAPTER 8

Knots

"GLAD IT WASN'T LIKE this yesterday! How was the new snowmobile?" asked Great Grandfather, passing a platter of blueberry pancakes. Outside, a blinding snowstorm had settled in after a bluebird day on Friday. The family loved snow machines and the winter before Dad had rented two Arctic Cats for the kids to begin riding on their own. Despite a hair-raising avalanche the year before, the two were undaunted and had begun talking about riding as soon as hunting season was over. On Christmas Day, they found a silver Polaris, wrapped in a big red bow, waiting for them in the garage.

Great Grandfather had contributed to the present and had been thoroughly briefed about the local test rides they'd made during the Holidays. When vacation was over, sports kicked in and both kids had been tied up for several weekends. A Friday teacher-in-service day had given the family its first chance to ride on Wolf Creek Pass.

"Fantastic!" exclaimed Sophia. "We took turns driving; it's a sweet machine!"

"It's quite a bit older than the ones Mom and Dad ride," said Juan, "but the engine's slightly bigger. Even with two of us on it, we can outrun them!" He chortled at the memory.

"Sounds wonderful, no trouble with avalanches?" The old man raised his eyebrows.

"As careful as Dad was, I think we all learned a lesson last winter," replied Sophia. "We stayed well clear of the steep slopes, although we still found some deep untracked powder!" she added with a grin.

"How'd you make out with Mrs. Martinez this morning?"

"Well, knowing we'd be coming here, I helped Juan with her breakfast," answered the girl. "We made scrambled eggs, sausage, and toast. She's always so cheerful. She told us about the time you came to deliver a dozen eggs and tripped on the doorstep, breaking every one of them on her kitchen floor! She said she could have whipped up a scramble right there on the floor except for the shells…" Both kids loved to gently tease their relative about things like this. He possessed a great sense of humor and it wasn't often they got one over on him.

"I'd rather not talk about that," he said with a sniff. "A board had come loose under the door and caught the toe of my boot." The twins winked at each other. Great Grandfather had maintained the widow's house for all the years since her husband died; there wasn't a loose board anywhere in the structure!

"Now, where was I when you were here last?" said he, changing the subject.

"Cuto had just addressed the warriors of Snorts Like A Bull in the kiva," Juan answered. He was particularly interested in the battles of their ancestors. "What kind of odds did they face?" he asked.

"There was a thinly spread population of more than 2,000 foreigners in the area, including Spaniards, their families and workers, soldiers, priests, and people of mixed blood marriages," replied Great Grandfather.

"That seems like a lot."

"Yes, but there were relatively few soldiers and they were spread out to fight the Apache and Navajo who were both pillaging the area. When Popé was released, he went to the Taos Pueblo and for the next five years he quietly recruited Indians in many pueblos to revolt. He was a charismatic leader, and decades of oppression had created enough hatred: the seeds were sewn to kill the Spanish. One amazing aspect of the uprising is that it was organized in secret across a large area: some pueblos joined in from nearly 200 miles away! The concept was for each pueblo to rise up and kill all the Spanish near it and then proceed to Santa Fe to wipe out the town.

"Popé was obsessed with confidentiality, because not all the pueblos were hostile to the conquistadors. It's alleged he killed his own son-in-law, fearful he would betray them. Four towns of the Tiwa, and all the Piro Pueblos, had been integrated into the Spanish culture. Had they learned of the conspiracy, they would have disclosed it to the Governor immediately, but it was not revealed. The revolt was planned for August 11, 1680."

"How in the world could he coordinate something like that?" wondered Juan. "You said some of the pueblos were almost 200 miles away; he had no means to communicate rapidly with them!"

"It was simple and ingenious," replied the old man. "Knotted ropes were sent to each pueblo. The first knot was untied on the day of the new moon, the day the last knot was untied was the day to rise up!"

CHAPTER 9

Discovered!

"Four days left," said Cuto, staring at the rope. "Are your men ready?" He was sitting with Swallow's grandson in a large room on the third floor of the pueblo.

"Yes, they've been assembling weapons and provisions. By tomorrow, all will be in order," answered Snorts Like A Bull.

"What of the women and children?"

"They leave in the morning for the cliff house of the Ancients. A few of the older men will go with them for protection," said the Indian.

"Good," replied the Aztec, imagining the sheer walls above and below the dwelling built into the cliff face five miles from his secret canyon. "It won't be the first time the Ancients provided protection for your pueblo."

"My grandmother told me about the time she fooled you and Ria," remarked the chief with a smile. Thinking back to the day Swallow had suddenly disappeared from the rim of the canyon, the old man grinned.

"We thought she'd fallen to her death. Then she giggled, from her position on the handholds below, but we still couldn't see her because of the slope of the rock. She played a wonderful trick on us!" He turned serious.

We've left men behind to guard our families and the horses, but Rutu, Necalli, Beast Blinder, and I will assist you in the assault on Santa Fe. We will each need a blanket to carry out my plan."

"I will have them brought immediately," said the Indian, wondering privately how a blanket could be turned into a weapon.

"Tomorrow we will leave for the town. When you attack at dawn on the fourth day, we will be ready." With this enigmatic remark, the white haired Aztec rose and headed for the ladders to find his men.

The next morning, as the women and children were leaving the pueblo, a rider came racing in from Santa Fe. He leaped from his horse and shouted for Snorts Like A Bull. When the leader ran up, the messenger blurted the news.

"The Tiwa captured two boys carrying knotted ropes. The Spanish are torturing them right now to learn what it means! Popé has sent messengers to every nearby pueblo. You are to attack tomorrow at dawn instead of the day after." The men nearby stared at him, stunned that the secret might have been had been discovered.

"I need a fresh horse. There are other pueblos to alert!" cried the man. A mount was quickly provided and the courier raced away. The Indians galvanized into action. One group was designated to enter Santa Fe at night and stampede the soldiers' horses. Another had been picked to destroy the gates into the walled plaza so the Spaniards couldn't barricade themselves inside. Both sorties had been planned for just before dawn, while the conquistadors slept. Now they had to carry out the operation a day early and against a population that would be on guard.

Cuto sent Rutu to tell Snorts Like A Bull the Aztecs were leaving immediately; when they heard the horses stampede the next morning, they'd join the attack. Within minutes the four were riding towards the Spanish town, several hours away. By evening, each was hidden in bushes or trees at four points bracketing the community. Strangely, it was quiet; the normal smell of cooking beans and tortillas carried on a gentle breeze. Stars sparkled above in the clear sky and the usual chill of the desert night fell over the area.

From his hiding place on a small hill, Rutu could see lights in buildings around the plaza and the figures of soldiers moving about inside. He was surprised. Either the Governor didn't believe there could be a serious threat, or the youths had died before revealing what the knotted ropes predicted. Beside him was a saucer-shaped hollow, 12 inches deep, which he'd made with his knife while there was still daylight. In it was laid wood for a fire. A heavy pack rested on the sand beside him and his loaded sling was stretched out, ready for instant use if the need arose.

The Aztec stretched out, hands under his head, and stared at the stars. He knew Cuto and the others were doing much the same thing; they were all waiting for the Indian attack on the horse herd—still hours away. He thought about Beast Blinder. The Crow was devoted to him and Lita, and had become an excellent horse trainer. He was now about 20 and slender, long black hair reaching almost to his waist. He dressed in the knee-high moccasins and loose cotton clothes of the Aztecs, but his darker skin and features set him apart. The quiet, brooding personality they had first known had disappeared, replaced by a lively spirit that made him a favorite with children wherever he went.

Twice a year Rutu and Beast Blinder traveled to Snarling Badger's village in the great valley bordered by jagged peaks. True to his promise years earlier, Snarling Badger maintained a teepee specifically dedicated to the Aztec's use. In the beginning Rutu and Beast Blinder were delivering buffalo runners and training Ute riders, but as time went by the three men became so close that the trips expanded to two or more weeks of riding, hunting and enjoying each other's company.

During the spring trip this year, Rutu had noticed the Crow warrior taking long walks with a beautiful Ute girl. In fact, Beast Blinder, using one pretext or another, had delayed their departure for a third week! Rutu suspected the desert might be losing one of its inhabitants to the mountains. It looked like he would be making the trip to see Snarling Badger alone in the future. Suddenly he sat up, startled by the sound of a dog barking. Glancing at the sky, he saw the faintest sign of light on the eastern horizon. The Indians would be launching their attack soon!

CHAPTER 10

Fire and Demons

In MINUTES RUTU HAD a small fire going in the pit. Around the edge he placed a handful of rocks, adding a few directly on the burning wood. From his sack he drew a clay jar, its narrow opening corked with a wood plug. Next he laid out a dozen squares of cloth cut from the Indian blanket he'd received. Feeding the fire, he used a pair of stout sticks to turn the stones over and over until they began to glow with heat. He carefully poured oil from the jar onto each piece of cloth until it was soaked through.

A horse whinnied behind the plaza. Then another. There was a shout and a musket shot. War cries erupted and hooves thundered as the Indians charged from the darkness into the large horse enclosure next to the plaza. There were more shouts and gunfire; then figures began streaming from the barracks into the plaza and running for the corral.

Suddenly, high overhead, a ball of fire appeared arcing down toward the plaza. It dropped onto the straw roof of a nearby building, igniting the material. This was the sign Rutu had been waiting for! Using two strong sticks for tongs, he picked up one of the red-hot stones and placed it on an oil-soaked piece of cloth, tied the cloth and hurled the bundle into the air with a mighty throw of his sling. The friction between the air on the outside and the heat from the rock inside, caused the cloth to burst into flame and the firebomb fell onto a pile of hay near the corrals, setting it ablaze.

By now Necalli and Beast Blinder were in action and screams from the terrified inhabitants filled the air as fireballs rained from the sky, igniting everything they touched. More war cries erupted as the second war party charged into Santa Fe, heading for the Plaza gate. They met a withering volley of musket fire and fell back, but not before one brave managed to throw a rope, weighted with a big rock, over the top pole of the gate. The force of the throw caused the rock to wrap itself twice around the pole; the brave turned his horse sharply away, trying to pull the gate off its hinges. The gate started to buckle, but the tension was too great and the pole snapped in two before the barrier broke. Soldiers on the inside immediately began piling boxes and bales inside the gate to prevent it from being breached.

Rutu threw his last fireball and reached into the sack. He pulled out a soft leather pouch of considerable size. From it he gently extracted the head skin of a jaguar, prepared and cured by his ancestor Itta nearly 150 years before. Each generation of the family had kept it soft and pliable, hidden except for special occasions. Slipping it over his head, he found he could see perfectly through the eyeholes, just as Cuto had described. The skin completely covered his head and fell over his shoulders and neck, giving him a savage appearance.

The sun was still below the horizon as Rutu descended into the burning town. Smoke from flaming roofs and dust from the Indian horses filled the air. People were running about, crying out in fear and calling for loved ones. Spanish residents fled toward the safety of the plaza, Indian inhabitants toward the hills and the pueblos. The plaza, surrounded on four sides by Palace, barracks, storerooms and stable, was a natural fort. Soldiers opened the gate a few feet and made a passage through the boxes for people to slip in. In the meantime the officers were organizing troops to make a counter-attack against the Indians. The situation was utterly chaotic, compounded by war cries from the braves and screams from the wounded.

Taking charge, the commander ordered men to the few unignited roofs of buildings around the Plaza. They kept up an irregular musket fire, which probably saved the plaza from being overwhelmed in the first hour. Officers retrieved a few horses from the stable, mounted, and ordered the gates cleared and opened. Three of them led 50 conquistadors, in lines of four abreast, followed by a group of 20 friendly Indian militiamen from the enclosure. Citizens fleeing to the safety of the Plaza scattered to the sides of the column, cheering as it passed.

Snorts Like A Bull's warriors gave way before the soldiers' formation and it advanced 200 yards before the Captain leading them inexplicably fell from his horse. His men rushed forward to find a stone deeply imbedded in his skull just above the nose; he was dead before he hit the ground! While they were examining the body, one lieutenant, then the other, dropped from their horses, similarly stricken. The soldiers looked wildly around, but in the smoke and dust there was nothing to be seen. A corporal organized the men into a loose oval formation to meet what they expected would be a head-on assault by the Indians. The men crouched, pikes and lances aimed outwards but nothing materialized out of the fog-like conditions.

A soldier threw hands to head and toppled backward, fatally struck by a rock hurtling through the air. Across the oval, another fell...then another...and another. The Indian militiamen, forming the backside of the oval, had bows at the ready, but no targets. One of them suddenly screamed in pain and collapsed, clutching a shattered shoulder.

"There," bellowed another. "Beside that house!"

"Where?" cried the man beside him.

"I saw a figure in the smoke!" They peered intently, bows at full draw, but a little puff of wind parted the smoke to reveal nothing. Another militiaman screamed and fell as his leg broke and gave way under him.

Firing off an arrow wildly, another man yelled, "There it is again!" "I saw something low moving through the smoke!" No sooner had he spoken than the bow fell to the ground from his broken right arm. Above the din, a militiaman shrilled with fear.

"It's a beast! A beast is stalking us in the smoke!" One of the conquistadors ran to him. He yelled at the frightened man.

"Get hold of yourself, it's the Indians racing around us on their horses!"

"Noooo…there it is again," shrieked the now terrified Tiwa, just as the Spaniard crumpled to the ground, blood spurting from his cracked skull.

"I saw it!" screamed another militiaman, staring in a different direction and pointing, bow forgotten. By now the entire militia group had become obsessed with the figure moving about in the smoke no more than 20 yards away. They peered, weapons forgotten, as their minds grappled with faint memories of a legendary man-beast that had once destroyed an Apache war party.

For a split second it materialized in the smoke, rushing at them, emitting savage roars and whirling one arm over its fearsome head. It was too much. The men broke and ran, straight into the backs of the soldiers at the other end of the oval. As the militia struggled to get past the conquistadors and away from the beast, the soldiers thought they were being attacked by the Pueblo Indians from behind. A melee ensued, men slashing at one another with sword, lance, tomahawk and knife. When it was over, a dozen militiamen were down plus an equal number of Spaniards. In complete panic, both sides fled, the soldiers back toward the Plaza and the remaining militia toward the hills.

CHAPTER 11

Questions

As the sun rose over the smoldering town, Rutu joined the others at a prearranged spot in the hills just outside, the jaguar head-skin safe in his pack. Cuto's eyes were lively but lines of weariness showed in his face.

"You handled it perfectly!" he exclaimed.

"I tried to do what you directed," replied Rutu, squatting beside him. "Leave most of the sling work to the three of you and concentrate on letting the Indians catch glimpses of me. It seemed to work."

"I've never seen anything like it!" exclaimed Necalli. "It was just the way Cuto has described the Apache fight. You were like a ghost moving around in the smoke!"

"You couldn't have timed the charge better!" Beast Blinder chuckled. "They were so scared that their minds couldn't have accepted it if you'd talked to them in a normal voice, much less roars from the apparition coming at them! Their desperation created such a fight with the soldiers that Snorts Like A Bull's men didn't have to attack. I don't think the Governor will risk another sortie. He lost at least half of his soldiers and all the militia!" Catching their horses, they went to meet Snorts Like A Bull.

"My men and I are grateful for your help," he said as they sat on a hill overlooking the town, smoke drifting up in lazy plumes from ruined houses. "We ran off the horse herd," he continued, "and the rain of fire distracted the soldiers and townspeople so much they didn't counter-attack. I seem to remember stories from my grandmother about fire from the sky…"

"It's an old trick my grandfather taught me," replied Cuto gravely. It was used to great advantage when the conquistadors invaded his country several lifetimes ago."

"My men also said the fleeing Tiwa were screaming about a beast coming after them," said the chief pointedly.

"We were using slings from hidden positions and they couldn't see the rocks coming. In all the dust and smoke, it was probably confusing for them," replied Cuto evasively.

"One of my men said they were so terrified they attacked their own allies trying to escape," persisted the Indian.

"Hmmm, perhaps they were completely unnerved by men falling around them without being able to see the enemy," said Cuto, refusing to bite. He changed the subject.

"I see Spanish people coming into Santa Fe and heading for the Plaza. Are you leaving them alone?"

"All the pueblos rose up today and attacked the invaders. They were to concentrate on the soldiers, but reports are coming in that many inhabitants were killed, including black robes, women and children. I have no desire to kill defenseless people, so we're letting them go to the Plaza. We've cut off the stream flowing into it; the Governor won't be able to stay there forever. Popé wants to see them retreat; killing them all will just bring an army against us."

"You have the situation in hand," said the old Aztec, rising and mounting his horse. "We've seen other warriors arriving to reinforce you, so we'll return to the canyon."

Snorts Like A Bull watched the four ride off, a quizzical smile on his face. He had personally talked to one of the captured militiamen. The fighter, wide eyed with terror, had sworn he saw a demon rushing at them through the smoke.

CHAPTER 12
Aftermath

"Wow!" cried Juan as Great Grandfather's eyes refocused from the reverie he often fell into while telling the family history. "That's an incredible story!"

"Cuto learned a great lesson when he attacked the Apache camp," explained the old man. "In circumstances of extreme stress and uncertain lighting, the brain can play amazing tricks on people."

"Yeah, if the militia had had a clear look at Rutu, without the distraction of the battle," offered Sophia, "they might have seen him for what he was: a man wearing a mask."

"Right," said the storyteller. "But when you consider the circumstances, combined with whispered rumors dating back almost 70 years, and the superstitions inherent in so many civilizations, it's no surprise those men panicked!"

"What happened to the people in the Plaza?" Juan wanted to know. "Didn't Popé want to kill all the Spanish?"

"Initially he did," acknowledged Great Grandfather. "But circumstances must have changed his mind. History reports that around 400 men, women, children and missionaries were killed in the initial uprising. Within three or four days, nearly 1,000 people were trapped in the Plaza at Santa Fe, cut off from water. It appears that Popé had nearly 2,000 men at his disposal and they essentially besieged the Plaza.

"About 10 days after the revolt started, the situation was getting desperate and the Governor had to do something to avoid being totally wiped out. He assembled his men and counter-attacked. The Pueblos suffered heavy losses, and the Governor took advantage of that and lead the rest of the people out of the Plaza and down the Rio Grande River toward El Paso. The Indians followed but didn't attack. In the end, some 1900 people escaped, including 500 Indian slaves." The twins sat for a moment, taking all this in.

"Surely the Spanish didn't take that lying down?" questioned Juan.

"No. The Governor, whose name was Antonio de Otermin, tried to take back the area a year later.

He brought a mixed group of nearly 300 Spanish and Indian soldiers to within about 80 miles of Santa Fe, but the Pueblos began assembling to fight and he withdrew. It wasn't until 1692, nearly 12 years later, that Spain took control of the region again."

"So, our family had a role in freeing the Pueblo Indians from Spanish rule," mused Sophia. "That makes me really proud!"

"Me too!" exclaimed Juan. He glanced out the window where the storm continued to rage, almost surprised he wasn't looking at scorching desert instead.

"What about Cuto and the others?" he asked.

"They returned to the canyon and resumed raising and training horses. Their reputation spread far and wide and for many years Indians showed up, some from hundreds of miles away, to trade for mounts. Even when tribes had their own herds, hunters or warriors would appear to acquire specialized animals, for which the family was famous.

"One amazing circumstance happened a few years after the Uprising: Cuto and Ria died peacefully on the same night in their sleep." He paused while they all considered the probabilities of that happening.

"That's not all," he continued. "Lita's daughter married an Aztec from the family's original village in Mexico. They had a daughter they called Ria, named after her great, great grandmother. The new Ria married Sand, the grandson of Snorts like a Bull; she carried on the horse training tradition and Sand split time between the canyon and the pueblo. They became grandparents to the boy named Tukor!"

"So the families of Ria and Swallow finally became related!" Sophia's eyes sparkled.

"Yes, nearly 150 years after Ria nursed Swallow back to health, her namesake married the Indian girl's descendant!" Great Grandfather smiled.

"What about the medallion?" asked Juan.

"When Lita was in her nineties, she passed it on to her granddaughter Ria, who eventually passed it to Tukor," replied the old man.

A week later, Great Grandfather surprised the twins with home-made sopapillas and honey-butter. As they happily munched on the delicious pastries, he settled back in the beautiful rocking chair.

"Now that we've filled in some background, let's return to the story of Tukor," he began, his face assuming the distant look which indicated he was returning to the past.

CHAPTER 13
Shadow

THE YOUTH'S EYES flew open in the dark, right hand instinctively moving to touch the animal curled against his leg. It came again: the low growl that had wakened him.

"What is it?" he whispered. He felt the wolf's body under his hand tense and another growl issued from its chest.

"Let's see what's out there," he breathed, reaching for his sling. He was on his feet in an instant, moving to the door of the adobe house as silent as a shadow, one hand resting lightly on the animal moving beside him. Outside, faint streaks of light showed above the towering canyon walls; dawn wasn't far off. The burbling of the creek a few yards away was cut by the sudden shrill of a sick foal housed with its mother in a corral nearby; simultaneously a snarl erupted from the creature beside him and it streaked toward the sound. A scream, almost human, pierced the air and the man knew exactly what had awakened his companion: a mountain lion was stalking the foal in the corral!

Snarling and hissing filled the air as he raced forward, loaded sling whirling around his head. Now the mare was snorting and stamping, frightened by the confrontation of predators, her terrified foal dashing about behind her. In the dark it was difficult to make out what was happening, but by bending low the young man was able to see a slight silhouette against the lightening sky above. On one of the upright posts, front paws resting on the top rail of the corral, was a large cougar spitting and hissing at the black animal crouched on the ground below. The cat's tail was lashing and the man knew it was ready to leap on its adversary, hesitating only because of the other's size. Straightening, the warrior narrowed his eyes and focused on the dim mass on top of the post before releasing the rock from his sling.

The centrifugal force generated by the five-foot weapon's powerful revolutions, released its missile at over 100 MPH. The rock struck the cat in the face with tremendous force, shattering its jaw and rupturing the windpipe. It fell to the ground and died under the jaws of the great black wolf.

"Leave it," said the warrior softly when the thrashing stopped. "That pelt will make a nice parfleche. Just maybe I can find a skilled seamstress in the village to do something with the head-skin," he added with a grin. The wolf backed off obediently, licking its bloody mouth.

"You stay here," said the man quietly. "I'm going to quiet the horses." He slipped through the poles and slowly approached the frightened animals pressed against the far side of the enclosure. "It's over," he murmured, letting the mare sniff the familiar scent of his hand. "Luckily, Shadow smelled the cat before he got into the corral. You might have held him off, but if the little one had bolted…there, there…good job mama…" There was movement in the dark.

"An intruder. I heard," said his father, Yellow Leaf, approaching the pen. "That companion of yours makes our job easy! Two cats in a year, not to mention the deer that don't dare come around our gardens any more!"

"To think he started out as such a little fellow," laughed Tukor, sliding through the corral poles. "I brought him home in the palm of my hand!" The wolf was instantly at his side, its back just below the level of his waist. Watched over incessantly by the boy who'd rescued him, the tiny pup had bonded so closely that the grown wolf, now five, rarely left his side. Somehow the horses realized the animal was a friend and were accustomed to its presence walking or running at their sides, no matter what the speed. Friends and family were accepted and strangers quietly tolerated. A low growl and raised hackles warned those deemed unfriendly, causing caution and a change of attitude: no one wanted to challenge the youth's fearsome guardian!

As dawn filled the sky, the two men bathed in the creek and then sat on well-worn tree stumps munching tortillas filled with vegetables and tender meat. Shadow lay beside Tukor, gnawing on a bone.

"I had word yesterday that a trader arrived at the pueblo," announced the older man. "He brought word that Crooked Horn is looking for 20 horses."

"We've certainly got 20 to trade, depending on what he's looking for," answered Tukor. "I'll ride over and ask them. It's odd," he mused, "we've traded a number of horses to Crooked Horn, but he's never been here. The traders say he likes our animals, so you'd think he'd come to see them first hand."

"My guess is he thinks it safer to stay away," his father chuckled, reflecting that the legends about the canyon had grown with time. "I'll go with you; I haven't been to the pueblo for a while."

That afternoon they approached the three-story building that Feather had introduced Cuto and Ria to so long ago. Built in the shape of a U, it was three stories high and colored a faint red. There were no doors or windows at ground level, preventing entry by an enemy; ladders gave access to the second story and from it to the third. Even from afar people could be seen moving about the upper levels and climbing or descending the ladders. A short distance behind the building was a rather steep hill with a flat top. Tukor knew that the plateau was covered with vegetable gardens watered by an ingenious system of canals fed by rainwater catch-basins. As they drew near, a lookout perched high on the building waved a greeting.

On the ground along the arms of the U were scattered numerous colorful blankets covered with vegetables, fruit, and a variety of goods for trade. At one end a pile of buffalo robes and several horses marked the presence of the trader who had been to Crooked Horn's camp.

A wizened old man sat leaning against the pile of robes, a tanned deerskin on the ground before him. On it were half a dozen small white carvings. Tukor's eyes narrowed as he slid from the back of his horse. The carvings looked similar to the ones his grandmother kept carefully wrapped in a beaded pouch among her belongings. She rarely brought them out, and then only in connection with questions about her great grandmother Lita's journey north with her brother.

"Where did you get these?" he asked, going to one knee to examine them.

"Far to the north," answered the old man, staring at the wolf that lay down beside the warrior. "From the people who live by the Great Water. The climate there is cool and damp; they trade for the buffalo robes I bring."

The young man studied him. Although dressed in the manner of desert people, with loose cotton shirt belted over pants tucked into high leather moccasins, he wore a bulky cap of black fur despite the warm temperature. His skin was darker than that of the Pueblos or Aztecs, and gray wisps of hair grew from his chin. A diagonal scar crossed the empty left eye socket and the good eye was slightly slanted.

"Is that your home?" queried Tukor, going to one knee, right hand resting lightly on Shadow, the left holding a small carving of what was clearly a wolf. The man hesitated for a moment.

"I have no home," he finally said enigmatically. "I travel among the peoples bringing things they value. I've just been to the Comanche, trading shells for these robes. Soon I'll be in the south trading Pueblo blankets for bracelets of green stones. By winter, I'll be in the north with these robes."

One needs good horses for all that travel," said Yellow Leaf, dismounting. "Yours look familiar somehow."

"Yes, I take care of them and they carry me and my goods faithfully over great distances," said the trader. "I bargained for them at this very pueblo last year. The owner said the stock is from a herd maintained by skilled horsemen in a great canyon."

"That's it; I thought the gray looked familiar," laughed Yellow Leaf. "I wanted to bring her to the canyon for training because she'd make an excellent buffalo runner, but I couldn't talk Elk's Tooth out of her! You must have offered him something special."

"I had to give three large ivory carvings for her," acknowledged the man. "So, you must be the men Crooked Horn wanted me to contact," he continued, raising the eyebrow over his good eye. "He's interested in 20 fast horses. He said he has more of these to barter," as he fingered a thick robe.

"So this is called 'ivory,?'" asked Tukor, examining the white carving. "Where does it come from?"

"It is from huge beasts that live in the Great Water," answered the old man. "Some of them have teeth this long." He spread his hands wide. "The people kill them for meat and make carvings from the teeth." Tukor stared, astonished that animals could have teeth that large.

"Your great, great grandmother learned of these people when she was a young woman," said his father. "She set out with her brother to find the Great Water but nearly died and had to winter where they encountered The Beast." Tukor nodded. The story was well known among the people in the canyon.

"Crooked Horn wants 20 fast horses," declared Yellow Leaf. "Did he say what for? Buffalo runners or war horses?"

"No. He just said, 'tell them I want swift horses,'" answered the trader. "He said he'd be camped near the canyon where the two rivers meet." He stared at them pointedly with his good eye. "Be careful, he's treacherous."

CHAPTER 14
Medallion

THREE DAYS LATER 20 young horses had been chosen from the herd, characterized by the promise of speed all had exhibited. The family decided Tukor would deliver them, accompanied by two riders from the village in the main canyon and several packhorses to carry the buffalo robes he would bargain for. The evening before his departure, his grandmother was unusually quiet. Her dark brown face was lined with wrinkles and her hair completely white, but her black eyes still warm and lively. Seated on a blanket, she waited as tortillas, vegetables, and meat were passed around and the final details of Tukor's trip had been discussed.

"I've had a dream," she finally announced in a clear voice during a break in the conversation. Every head turned toward her.

"A dream, Grandmother?" said Tukor. She looked at him.

"Yes, you were in great danger. I saw long lances, strange beasts, water, and billowing clouds. I woke up and knew it was time." She lifted a hand to a leather cord around her neck and pulled a round piece of silver from beneath her blouse. It was about four inches across and inscribed with strange symbols. A one-inch square hole was cut in the middle. The leather cord was smooth and deep brown from countless years of handling. Ria held the medallion out to the youth.

"I've worn this since I was about your age. The time has come to pass it on to you as the youngest family member. You must wear it always, for it possesses a great secret and our family is pledged to care for it until the secret is revealed. Each year, on the longest day and on the shortest day, gaze through it at the rising sun. Perhaps something will be revealed to you, although it hasn't been to me. If danger threatens, it will warn you.

"You're skilled in the use of the sling and have been taught to weave the armor shirt. These also are part of the instructions given by our dying ancestor Qist to his son Adzul during the battle for Pattiti in ages past. Have them with you wherever you travel." She leaned back and stared steadily at her great grandson. He ran a finger over the markings cut in the silver.

"How can it be so light for its size?" he exclaimed.

"I don't know, but it's never hurt my neck, nor has the cord worn out," she replied. The young man stared at the silver for many minutes before slipping the cord over his head.

"I am honored to accept the family heritage," he said softly.

CHAPTER 15
Treachery

Five days later, the little band of horses and three riders approached their destination in the vast prairie they'd been traversing. Two rivers had cut wide valleys in the terrain and joined to carve a great Y-shaped canyon stretching in an easterly direction. As they approached the northern valley, a cluster of about thirty teepees came into view in a cottonwood grove on the far bank of the river to their left.

"That must be Crooked Horn's camp," called Tukor from the front of the herd, swiveling on his mount to address the two men at the back. "Just where the trader said it would be."

"I hope they have fresh meat," moaned Zolin. "I'm getting tired of dried beans and corn!"

"If you'd been more accurate with that bow, we might have had antelope steaks last night," laughed Ohtli. Just 18, and a still inexperienced hunter, the younger man had successfully approached the only antelope they'd seen for three days, lying low along his horse's back. Unfortunately, he'd raised his head too soon, spooking the animals immediately. His hasty long-range shot was far short of the mark.

Riders began streaming from the village to meet them, and the travelers were accompanied for the last mile by a large group of Comanche men and boys. All of them studied the horses intently, talking among themselves, but kept their distance from the leader with the large black wolf trotting beside his bay stallion. On a grassy flat a little way from the teepees Tukor raised a hand and his companions backed off, allowing the horses to graze. Within minutes, several more riders approached from the camp. At the front was a smallish man mounted on a white mare.

Like the others, this man was naked from the waist up, clad in breechcloth and moccasins. His black hair was parted down the middle and fashioned into two long braids falling in front of his shoulders. The skin along the part in his hair had been dyed bright red and a length of hair on the top of his head had been braided into a thin strand about 8" long. From his pierced ears dangled bits of colored shell and tattoos covered his upper arms. But, despite the hand raised in greeting, the impassive face with its cold black eyes was anything but friendly.

"I see the trader delivered my message," said Crooked Horn in the language common to the Southwestern peoples.

"Yes, he said you would trade buffalo hides for swift horses and we chose 20 two-year-olds that show promise of great speed," replied Tukor.

"They come from the canyon?" asked the Comanche.

"Yes, out of the herd developed by my family," said Tukor. The chief's eyes widened slightly.

"I didn't think one of the family members would bring the animals. In the past, you've sent others," said Crooked Horn.

"In the past, you've sent hides and agreed to have some of your warriors meet our men closer to Santa Fe. It seems our horses have always been satisfactory, but this time you just sent a request," said Tukor levelly. Ignoring the remark, the Indian moved among the horses, eyeing each closely for several minutes. At length, he issued a command and several men rode off to the village. He motioned toward a flat area a few yards away.

"Let us conduct our business there." Leaving his men with the horses, Tukor rode to where Crooked

Horn had dismounted. One of the braves spread a blanket on the ground and the two men sat facing each other. Shadow settled down beside Tukor's right hip.

"I've sent my men for the buffalo robes," announced the chief. "Afterwards you and your men will join us for a feast to celebrate the transaction. Tukor nodded his head, acutely aware that he hadn't been offered the minimum courtesy of a pipe ceremony, nor anything to eat, as was customary in friendly dealings among the tribes. In fact, several armed warriors had ridden up and dismounted behind Crooked Horn. They stood behind the chief, each holding a lance. All at once, the Aztec felt a strange sensation on his chest. The medallion had become hot.

Having left his weapons and armor shirt on the packhorse, Tukor was unarmed, save the knife in its scabbard at his back and the sling around his waist; neither of which could be brought to use quickly. He gazed at the Comanche and the warning of the old trader came to mind. Something was very wrong, but it defied reason. Surely Crooked Horn understood his access to fine horses would be denied forever if he harmed the men in any way, to say nothing of retribution from the Aztecs and their allies. What had gotten into the man? Resting one hand on the wolf, he felt tension—Shadow sensed danger.

"I see your men are bringing the robes," he said calmly as riders leading two packhorses appeared behind the chief. When they arrived, he rose. "I'd like to examine the robes." Crooked Horn waved a hand in acknowledgement. Although the four men behind the chief seemed relaxed, Tukor could see knuckles standing out on the hands gripping the lances, indicating the warriors were poised to use their weapons. Walking to the pack animals, wolf at his side, he carefully examined the hides and returned to stand before the chief.

"The robes are in excellent condition, your hunting must have been good," he said.

"Yes," acknowledged Crooked Horn, having to lift his eyes because Tukor had not resumed his seat.

"Three more horses loaded with skins like these will complete the trade," announced Tukor.

"Two is my offer," growled the chief. Both of them knew the proposal was an insult for the quality of horses delivered. Normally, there was considerable bargaining in a transaction of this kind, often extending for hours over food and drink, but Crooked Horn's tone of voice and demeanor indicated this was not to be the case.

"Very well, I'll return the horses to the canyon and we can do business another time, but you will have to visit us," said Tukor calmly. He turned to go, the medallion nearly burning his skin. Two Indians blocked the way, lances pointed at his chest. They'd come up so silently he'd been unaware of their presence, focused as he was on the chief. Without warning, both lunged forward with killing thrusts aimed at his abdomen. No one was prepared for what happened next.

There was a blindingly intense flash of light and both lances vaporized in white smoke, leaving the two warriors screaming in agony and staggering backward with severely burned hands. With a fearsome snarl, the black wolf launched itself at the nearest one and would have savaged his throat but for a sharp command from Tukor. The man sprawled on his back, the great animal standing over him, teeth bared, emitting fearsome growls.

Turning, the Aztec beheld Crooked Horn on his feet. Gone was arrogance and malevolence, naked fear in his eyes. Behind him, the four men stood poised to flee, lances forgotten, shock on their faces as ancient legends flickered in their minds.

"I came to trade horses," said Tukor simply, despite his own awe over what had occurred. "Why did you wish us harm?" There was a long silence as the Comanche tried to compose himself.

"The Comanche rule this prairie and fear no man. We've defeated the invaders from the south. We've conquered and enslaved all the peoples who've come into our land. We take what we want," the chief said honestly. "In foolishness, I decided the whispers from the past about your canyon were the imaginings of weak Apache. No longer would I trade; I would take your horses and then your herd."

"For many, many years Indians have come great distances to trade for our horses and have always been fairly treated," replied Tukor, noting that the medallion was cool again. "Long ago some tried to cheat us, but not many survived. Powerful forces protect my family, as you have seen; beware, lest you risk your life and those of your warriors," he added.

"You and your men are welcome in our village," said Crooked Horn, although his eyes were still fearful. "We will have a great feast tonight. Stay and hunt with us for a few days, then return home with many buffalo robes."

CHAPTER 16

Comanche Empire

"Whoa," said Juan. "That would put a stop to anyone aiming to stealing horses from the family!" Another week had gone by and the twins were settled comfortably in Great Grandfather's kitchen, enjoying ginger cookies and a mixture of hot milk and coffee.

"Could Crooked Horn really have been that arrogant?" asked Sophia. "Were the Comanche so powerful?"

"More powerful than people really comprehend," replied Great Grandfather. "Originally, they were part of the Shoshone nation living in what is now southern Wyoming. Moving south, probably following the buffalo migrations, they had become a separate people by around 1700. While they probably acquired a few horses from our family, the Popé Revolt gave them access to hundreds of horses that had escaped into the wild.

"The acquisition of increasing numbers of such animals transformed the Comanche into perhaps the finest fighting horsemen in the world and caused them to become one of the great Indian nations in this country. From the early 1700's to the 1870's they operated in the area called 'Comancheria,' which included Texas, eastern New Mexico, and southern Kansas, measuring almost 400 by 500 miles! They were divided into many sub-tribes, each autonomous, although several would come together at times to raid into Mexico or Texas. For over a century they terrorized everyone in proximity to Comancheria.

"Within Comancheria was an area known as the Llano Estacado, a trackless plateau primarily in west Texas larger than the state of Indiana. It is one of the largest tablelands in the United States and was reported by early travelers, including the conquistadors, as having absolutely no distinguishing features for countless miles in any direction. It was in this vast wilderness that a few Comanche bands operated with absolute impunity. Anyone venturing into the area was subject to becoming hopelessly lost and succumbing to the elements, or being attacked and slaughtered by the Indians when they least expected it.

"Most of the bands in the Llano Estacado belonged to the Quahadi tribe of Comanche, possibly the fiercest group in that nation. So remote were they that the outside world knew little about them until the early 19th Century. It was to a band of this tribe that Crooked Horn belonged. More than 70 years later, the great Comanche leader, Quanah Parker, would emerge from another Quahadi band in the Llano Estacado."

"That name sounds familiar," said Juan, looking at his sister. "Didn't we study him in our Southwestern History class?"

"Yes," affirmed Sophia. "If I remember right, he was the son of a Texas girl captured by the Comanche. She grew up in the tribe, married a warrior, and had two boys, one named 'Peanuts.' He died of sickness, but the other became a great fighter."

"Good memory," said the old man. "The older boy was Quanah. He was considered one of the greatest Comanche fighters, but after his surrender to the U.S. Army in 1875, he adapted to the Texans' way of life and became successful in the cattle business. In time he built a large house in Texas, and entertained a number of great American leaders. In his time, Crooked Horn had every reason to be arrogant, since the Comanche dominated the entire region."

"Sounds like he finally became honest with Tukor," remarked Juan.

"The Indians were superstitious," noted Great Grandfather. "Faced with the awesome phenomenon he had just observed, the chief knew he was in the presence of someone more formidable than he. He then had no reason to lie."

"Wouldn't he have wanted Tukor out of there?" asked Juan. "Why invite him to stay and offer him a feast?"

"He probably wanted to regain favor with him," guessed Sophia.

"You're right," their relative smiled. "Why risk anything worse happening by further offending Tukor? It was much safer to extend hospitality and try to gain a powerful friend. The invitation changed Tukor's life."

CHAPTER 17

The Slave

BY NIGHTFALL A TEEPEE had been prepared for the visitors, flanked by great piles of hides…their packhorses would be heavily loaded on the trip home. While buffalo meat was roasting over cooking fires, the Aztec horses were paraded through the village for everyone to see. Many two and three-year-old children were lifted onto their backs for a few steps; at the age of four they would be riding an old, gentle horse and by five they would have a mount of their own…six-year-olds began riding herd on the village's ponies.

In the evening a great bonfire was lit and feasting and dancing continued well into the night. Tukor and his men were given places of honor beside Crooked

Horn; however, the warriors maintained a discreet distance, clearly apprehensive of the dangerous power demonstrated out on the prairie. At one point, a bold toddler escaped his mother and wandered over to where Tukor was sitting before anyone could stop him. In stunned silence the people watched to see what would happen, fearful of both magic and the black wolf lying beside the man. When the Aztec lifted the child to his lap, tickling his tummy, and the wolf added a lick that elicited delighted giggles, there was a visible release of tension from the surrounding crowd.

As the festivities continued, Tukor noticed slaves dragging logs to the bonfire, bringing meat to the women for cooking, and collecting bones tossed randomly about by the Comanche. Characterized by dejection and fear, they were of all ages and included men, women, and children. Every one of them was scantily clad, or naked, with backs and limbs scarred from whippings. He knew the Indians customarily made slaves of people they captured, but he had never been exposed to the brutal treatment of such prisoners. During the evening he saw several kicked or beaten for no apparent reason, although most were adept at dodging out of the way before serious damage was done.

One man, however, caught his attention. He was slightly shorter than the Indians and had their brown skin and black hair, but his slanted eyes were markedly different. He held his head high and walked with a more purposeful step. New wounds on his back indicated ongoing abuse from his captors; from his undefeated posture, Tukor guessed they hadn't been able to break his spirit. He looked strangely familiar, although the Aztec knew he'd never seen the man before.

The next morning Crooked Horn invited the visitors to a demonstration of Comanche skills. Seated on robes, they watched braves ride by at a run, dropping to the offside of their horses as they passed so they were completely shielded from the observers, save for one foot showing on the animal's back, which prevented them from falling off. Boys ran their ponies past, leaning off to pluck a small bowl from the ground. Arrows were fired with deadly accuracy from under the necks of running horses into both stationary and moving targets. Roping demonstrations were given, with one rider chasing another to lasso his horse.

Then it was Tukor's turn. The Comanche watched intently as he lifted his shirt, briefly exposing the medallion, to unwrap his five-foot sling. There were murmurs as he set the weapon whirring around his head, and exclamations of surprise as the buffalo rib thirty yards away suddenly shattered under the impact of the hurtling rock. Next, he had one of the warriors toss a rock in the air and sent it spinning away with a direct hit. The men watching grunted in appreciation. But it was his skill and accuracy while mounted on a racing buffalo runner that got their attention. Time

after time, and from all distances, he sent rocks crash-
ing into six-inch targets as he thundered past. Then he
duplicated the performance with bow and arrow. The
warriors were impressed: horsemanship and weapon
skills were highly valued.

When he returned to sit beside Crooked Horn,
Tukor glimpsed the slave with the slanted eyes watching
him from beside a nearby teepee. As their eyes met, a
woman appeared behind the man, stick of firewood
raised above her head. As the blow fell, he neatly spun
and grabbed the piece of wood from her hand before
it touched him. Dropping it on the pile stacked beside
the tent, he turned and walked away.

Tukor joined Crooked Horn on an antelope hunt
that afternoon, but he couldn't get the slave out of his
mind. They successfully approached the antelope by
lying along the backs of their horses to mask their
presence. They gave chase when the fleet pronghorns
suddenly sped away, the Comanche drawing his bow
and the Aztec whirling his sling. Tukor's buffalo runner was edging ahead of the Indian's mustang as both
missiles were launched. Two antelope tumbled in the
long grass, one with an arrow through its neck and
the other with a crushed skull. As they returned to
the village, antelope slung across their horses' with-
ers, it came to him: the slave bore a resemblance to
the old trader with the ivory carvings. That evening

he asked the Comanche leader where they had captured the man.

"The Comancheros traded him to us," replied Crooked Horn. "They got him from the Navajo, who said he was nothing but trouble because he was always trying to escape. He's young and strong and we got him for practically nothing. To flee in the prairie is useless: he'd soon die from the elements, if we didn't track him down first and roast him alive."

"His appearance is not quite that of an Indian," observed Tukor.

"We noticed," replied the chief, "but the Comancheros paid no attention to it: he was just property to trade. It's odd that you mention it."

"Why?" asked the Aztec.

"During the past three summer moons the old trader with one eye, who carried my message to you, has tried to buy him. One Eye offers many shells and carvings, but the old women won't let the slave go. He's a good worker, and the only one they haven't been able to break. They enjoy trying to beat him into submission as they do all the others we give them. He's tough," added Crooked Horn with grudging admiration for the man's bravery.

Talk soon turned to horses, a favorite topic among the Comanche. The leader was keenly aware that Tukor's buffalo runner had led the chase for the antelope and offered additional robes for him. The owner politely declined.

"That horse has been in training for over a year to hunt buffalo, unlike the young horses you requested," he explained. "He's promised to a Ute from the north." There was a flash of anger in Crooked Horn's eyes, which he quickly hid. There was no point in offending his powerful guest; nevertheless, he was determined to have the stallion.

CHAPTER 18

Consummate Horsemen

"AFTER THE INCIDENT with the lances?" cried Juan. "You've got to be kidding! Crooked Horn was going to try to take the horse?" The twins were reluctantly getting into their coats after the morning's tale.

"You've no idea how important horses were to the Comanche," replied Great Grandfather. "By this time, around 1800, they were far ahead of the northern tribes, both in use and understanding of the animals. Wild horses abounded in the plains, descendants of those introduced by the conquistadors three centuries earlier and the Comanche were skilled at gathering and taming them. Proficient ropers, they could have a wild mustang caught and gentled for riding within a matter of hours. They were the first to fight from horseback, long before the other Indians progressed from battling on foot. Obviously, this gave them a tremendous advantage over their enemies.

"In addition, they became skilled horse breeders—something few, if any, Plains Indians practiced. Crooked Horn would have been well aware that our family had developed and maintained a large herd for a long time. His interest was not only in animals for riding, but to breed with his own herd. Within 25 years of Tukor's visit the combined bands of Comanche owned thousands upon thousands of horses. A mere warrior might have three times the number of animals that a chief on the northern plains would own."

"Who were the Comancheros?" asked Sophia.

"I'm glad you asked, because they're usually misunderstood," responded the old man. "Most people consider them Mexican traders, or renegades, but they were really New Mexican traders: descendants of the early Spanish who arrived with the conquistadors in places like Santa Fe. The Comanche became their favorite customers because they liked to barter: willing to exchange prisoners they hadn't killed for gold, weapons, or other goods. The Comancheros developed a brisk business in human trafficking as first the Mexicans, and later the Americans, came to realize that family members could be ransomed from the Comanche."

"How did Crooked Horn try to get the stallion?" asked Juan.

"That's for next week," grinned Great Grandfather as he opened the door. "Don't freeze on the way home, it's cold out there!"

CHAPTER 19

Tikaani

THAT NIGHT TUKOR WARNED Zolin and Ohtli to be alert for anyone approaching the teepee. He suspected that the Comanche, though fearful of openly confronting them, might try to steal the stallion under cover of dark. He was well aware that one of the principal preoccupations of the Plains Indians was stealing horses from other tribes. The practice had become almost an art form. In addition to running off whole herds, warriors were adept at sneaking into villages in the dark of night and taking mounts staked right beside the owners' lodges. It was not uncommon for a sleeping brave to have a rope around his wrist stretching to a favorite war horse picketed just outside. Following the same practice, Tukor staked the bay alongside the teepee and tied a leather rope from its neck to his arm. Even so, he might have lost the horse but for Shadow.

In the middle of the night the wolf's head came up and a deep growl rumbled in its throat. Tukor was instantly awake and on his feet. He had deliberately left the entry flap thrown back, but the sky was overcast and he could see nothing. The cool medallion meant there was no danger to him; it was the horse they were after. In an instant he and the wolf were outside, standing by the stallion. It gave a little snort of acknowledgement as his familiar hand rubbed its nose. When another menacing growl emerged from Shadow, there was a tiny sound on the ground to the right. Tukor grinned. Peerless thieves that they were, the Comanche had been crawling on their bellies toward the horse, leaving no silhouette to be seen against the background even though it was almost pitch black. But for the warning from his companion, the bay stallion might have been long gone by morning, despite the leather strap. He sensed they were withdrawing, having heard the growl, although he could see nothing. In normal circumstances, they might have stayed in place until he went back to sleep, but the presence of the wolf and the incident with the lances dictated they leave him alone. Nevertheless, he decided to stay beside his horse for the rest of the night.

It was not more than an hour later when Tukor felt Shadow stir beside him. Another rumble came from the wolf, but this time it was much softer, indicating whatever was out there was not necessarily dangerous. The man sat up, peering into the darkness. A whisper came, so soft he could barely make it out.

"I mean no harm."

"Then why do you approach in the dark?" replied the Aztec in a low voice.

"I had to wait until all were asleep," said the voice. "There was no other time to speak with you."

"Who are you?"

"I am named Tikaani, but they call me Slant Eyes." Suddenly Tukor knew who was speaking.

"The old women beat you," he stated.

"Yes, but their strength is gone and they can't hurt me," came the answer. Remembering some of the fresh wounds on the man's back, Tukor had his doubts but pressed on.

"Why have you come?" he asked.

"It's the wolf," answered the slave. "He's a sign, a sign of freedom. You are to take me with you when you leave." Tukor's eyes went wide in the dark.

"I'm to take you with me? Crooked Horn said the old trader tried to buy you but the women wouldn't let you go. Why will they let me have you?"

"They won't," came the answer. "But the chief can order it and they have to obey. You'll find a way.

Now I must to return before they wake and find me gone. They'll cut off one of my hands if they think I tried to escape."

"Wait," whispered Tukor urgently. "Why do you think Shadow is a sign of your freedom?"

"Because 'Tikaani' means wolf," said the man as he slipped away.

CHAPTER 20

Wager

IN THE MORNING, Tukor called on Crooked Horn. Accompanied by several warriors, the chief was sitting in the sun on a buffalo robe. All were reclined against willow backrests, chewing buffalo ribs. The visitor thought he saw a flicker of anger in Crooked Horn's eyes as he approached, quickly replaced by a faint smile. The plan to steal the stallion had failed, and the Comanche didn't dare openly challenge his guest's magic. Instead, he waved a hand for Tukor to join them and gestured toward the bowl of ribs. After gnawing away for some minutes, the younger man spoke.

"I've been thinking about the stallion. No doubt you would like to have his blood running in your herd."

Watching closely, Tukor saw the Comanche's eyes light up before he casually shrugged his shoulders.

"You said the horse was promised to a Ute."

"Yes, but he really wanted a black still in training. Given the choice, he'll gladly wait for that animal if it's offered." Crooked Horn leaned forward, prepared to bargain.

"I'll add another pack horse load of robes," he declared.

"The horse is easily worth twice that, as you know," replied Tukor casually. "But I have another idea that might interest you. A race between my bay stallion and your white mare." The Comanche sat straight up. There was nothing the Plains Indians liked more than a horse race, unless it was the betting that went along with it.

"Terms?" he asked.

"My horse against the two colts staked behind your lodge." The chief's face remained impassive, but he was elated. He could replace the two colts in one season by breeding the stallion to his mares. Before he could accept, however, Tukor added calmly, "and the slave with the slanted eyes."

"What?" replied the startled Comanche. "You want the strange slave as well?" If he lost, he knew that depriving the old ones of their worker could cause great difficulty with all the women in the village. Whether the warriors admitted it or not, women completely controlled the atmosphere and comfort inside the home; and the old women had a strong influence on the younger wives.

"Yes," explained the Aztec. "Two colts hardly equal a trained stallion, but I need a strong worker at home; such a man could be of value to me."

"I'll offer any other two from among the slaves," the chief said. Tukor got to his feet.

"If the terms aren't acceptable," he answered smoothly, "we'll begin loading our horses." Crooked Horn was trapped. Pride wouldn't let him refuse the wager in front of his men and he desperately wanted the bay stallion. He reminded himself that no one had ever beaten his white mare.

"Agreed," he growled. "We'll race in the cool of the evening."

This announcement was accompanied by grunts of approval as the warriors rose to begin soliciting bets. Word of the race spread through the village like wildfire. The interest was intense; there was nothing like a horse race to enliven the routine of daily life. The chief's mare was one of the fastest horses in the herd and her backers had to offer two-to-one odds to attract bets against her. Warriors in need of knives, bows, or lances chose the stranger with his stallion. Women put up beautiful buckskin shirts, moccasins, and cooking pots in wagers with each other. Even the children bet, matching any sort of personal object with each other. All afternoon, the sound of haggling resonated among the lodges as people vied for better terms on their bets.

Crooked Horn spent the time painting a buffalo head, with one horn twisted askew, on each hindquarter and shoulder of the mare. He used yellow paint, and enclosed the drawing with a circle of black. Each of the horse's eyes was circled in black and there were alternating stripes of yellow and black on both sides of her neck. As he worked, a plan began to form in his mind.

Tukor spent the afternoon wandering around the village answering questions about his horse from numerous clusters of people. In the process he noted Crooked Horn painting his horse and wondered about it; normally an Indian horse was only painted for battle, but perhaps the chief wanted a warlike frame of mind for the race. At a lodge on the outskirts of the village Tikaani was at work gathering firewood. Tukor paid no attention to the slave, but he was certain the man had spotted him and knew about the race. He steered clear of his own lodge, where Zolin and Ohtli were tying up bundles of buffalo robes for easy loading onto the packhorses staked nearby. He had told them to be ready to depart the moment the race was over. The stallion grazed peacefully on a short lead near them and the great wolf was stretched out a few feet away.

Crooked Horn finished painting his horse and sought out the medicine man, who lived in a lodge a little way outside the village. He was a strange one, old and stooped, with bright eyes that seemed to see right through you. Most of the band gave him a wide berth, although they kept him well supplied with food and firewood because of his healing powers. Several gravely wounded warriors had fully recovered after his ministrations and at least two children were restored to life after what had appeared to be fatal illnesses. Such a man was to be revered…and feared. As the chief scratched on the skin over the entrance, a strangely high-pitched voice sounded from within.

"You've come for protection from the trader's magic." The startled leader didn't dare ask how the other knew his errand.

"Yes," he said. "We are racing this evening."

"It's not the race you want favor for," came the voice. "It's to steal the piece of silver he wears and acquire its power."

"Yes," replied the chief.

"Come in; I've been waiting for you."

CHAPTER 21
The Race

When Crooked Horn emerged from the medicine man's lodge, the sun was close to the western horizon and the air had cooled considerably. He hurried toward his teepee, fingers briefly touching a small leather pouch now held against his neck by a leather cord. A group of warriors had gathered near his horse and he signaled as he approached that it was time for the race. One hurried to find Tukor and the others began to move toward the edge of the village.

"Bring your horse," the messenger announced to the Aztec, who was watching a group of young children chase a rolling hoop with their sticks. "It's time."

Tukor reluctantly turned away and strolled towards his dwelling, mindful of people hurrying toward the starting area. As he approached, Shadow rose and came forward to greet him, mouth open in a toothy grin. The man stroked the wolf's head and uttered a short command for him to remain where he was.

"Be careful," warned Zolin. "The chief spent a long time in a strangely painted lodge outside the village. I'm not sure you can trust him."

"Load the robes on the horses while the village is distracted and have Ohtli take them across the river," said Tukor. "You stay with Shadow and an extra horse for the slave. The mare is fast, but we picked my buffalo runner for training because of his exceptional speed and I'm confident we'll win. I want to leave immediately after the race because I think they'll attack tonight if we stay."

"I'll keep the horses hidden in the trees on the far bank," said Ohtli.

"No, take them over the ridge and out of sight," answered Tukor. "The minute you see us start across the river, head for home. We'll find you in the dark." The other nodded his understanding.

Mounting the stallion, Tukor rode slowly toward the crowd assembled beyond the lodges. Every eye was on him as he approached and he could see heads bent together in discussions, which he knew were about last-minute wagers. Well to one side stood a stooped figure pointing a stick at him, on which was mounted the head of a raven. He noticed the medallion was warm, but attributed it to general hostility directed at him out of fear, particularly from the warriors.

"That boulder is the turning point," announced Crooked Horn, gesturing to the right at a large rock sticking above the grass about half a mile away. "The race will begin and end here." The white mare, feeling the excitement, was prancing and ducking her head, trying to spin around and around. Distracted by thoughts that a long race was advantageous, due to the bay's stamina, Tukor noticed the chief did not allow the horse to spin, but positioned it in such a way its left side was never exposed. The Aztec thought it was for the purpose of a sudden start and he was partially correct: with no warning Crooked Horn suddenly sped off. Anticipating such a move, Tukor was only a jump behind.

The mare was fast and the Aztec was content to keep his horse slightly behind, just off her right hip. He knew the time to make his move was well after they had turned and headed toward the finish line. The stallion was running smoothly and comfortably, sensitive to the rider's body and trained to respond to any change of its position. The horses thundered toward the rock, dust rising behind them.

When they were within 100 yards of the boulder, Crooked Horn leaned slightly to the left and slowed his horse just enough for the bay to draw even. The Comanche had the inside position for the turn and Tukor thought he was trying to force the buffalo runner wide and gain a greater lead. Then the mare slowed even more and the stallion moved ahead. Suddenly the medallion was hot and Tukor glanced back to see Crooked Horn whirling a leather lasso that he had hidden under his left leg. The Aztec desperately swung the stallion to the right, but it was too late: the rope caught the animal's left front leg in full stride and pulled the horse off balance, pitching it forward in a cloud of dust to roll completely over its rider.

Crooked Horn was off his horse in a flash racing toward the still form of his opponent, a knife in his right hand and his left hand gripping the amulet provided by the medicine man for protection. The round piece of silver had popped from under the victim's shirt and lay on the dirt beside his neck; a knife thrust through the abdomen to kill him slowly and a flick of the blade through the strap would give the chief the power he craved. With a smile he stepped forward and directed a slashing blow at the Aztec's stomach.

The blade never met skin. Flame erupted from the medallion and enveloped the knife! The Comanche screamed in fear and jumped back trying to drop the weapon, but he couldn't unclench his fingers. A thin stream of fire connected him to the medallion; to his horror, flame began creeping up his arm, scorching the skin and causing intense pain. Eyes bulging, he tried to pull away, but it was useless: the fire was like a steel band connecting him to the silver disc. When the flame reached his shoulder, he passed out and fell to the ground; the stream of fire immediately disappeared.

A wet tongue licking his face brought Tukor to consciousness. Shadow had somehow known he was in trouble and raced to his side. He struggled to a sitting position, shuddering at the effort: the right side of his chest throbbed in agony from three broken ribs. A few feet away Crooked Horn lay unconscious, his right arm horribly burned, a knife still gripped in his hand and a small burn mark on his neck where the protective amulet had rested. Nearby, their horses grazed peacefully. Clearly something dramatic had happened while he was unconscious. He touched the medallion. It was cool, save for a small hot area bordering the square hole. Before he had time to consider this, he heard voices.

A crowd of Indians was approaching on foot, preceded by warriors on horseback. They had all seen the cloud of dust when the stallion fell and then a brilliant display of light. The men rode up, took in the scene at a glance, and backed well off. They wanted no part of whatever had harmed their leader. Getting slowly to his feet Tukor faced them, the wolf at his side.

"Crooked Horn dealt treacherously," he began. "He concealed a rope and brought my horse down as we approached the rock. Apparently he wanted more than the horse: you can see the knife he still clutches." He turned and walked slowly to the stallion, forcing himself to mount, though he almost fainted from the pain. He stopped in front of the crowd and gestured at their fallen leader who was starting to moan.

"We came in peace with our horses. You did not deal with us peacefully, but the protection of my family is not limited to our canyon walls. Beware, lest you think to test it yet again." The shock and fear on all the faces was evidence they heeded his words. Only when he was well on his way to the village did they dare move forward to tend Crooked Horn.

Zolin, who had come with the others, rode up beside the haggard Tukor and reached out a hand to support him.

"No," gasped the Aztec. "We must show them no sign of weakness. Find the slave and follow me across the river." As they approached the lodges, a stooped figure watching them from behind a cottonwood tree turned and limped slowly toward a distant painted teepee.

CHAPTER 22

Wisdom

Juan and Sophia stared at Great Grandfather in stunned silence.

"A stream of fire…" exclaimed Sophia, wide-eyed.

"That's amazing!" cried Juan, fingering the silver under his shirt. "We've never seen the medallion do anything like that."

"It's a mystery," acknowledged the old man. "The medallion has immense power and it seems to react according to circumstances. Simple warmth alerted you to the cougar; heat saved you under the avalanche, and searing heat like that of an acetylene torch freed you from the tree in the river. All Wearers have experienced its protection from time to time, occasionally in most unusual ways, as you've heard."

"Has it done anything else so dramatic?" Juan wanted to know.

"You'll have to wait and see," grinned his relative.

"Did Crooked Horn lose his arm?" asked Sophia.

"No, but it was never quite the same," answered Great Grandfather. "Two years later, a Comanche warrior showed up in the canyon, close to death. He was the only survivor of an attack, far out on the Llano Estacado, by the Apache against a small trading party Crooked Horn had sent to Santa Fe.

"This man had been badly wounded and barely survived the wilderness. He forced himself to quell his great fear of the legends and seek help. The village took him in and nursed him back to health. Word was sent to Yellow Leaf and, when the man had recovered, the leader paid a visit to question him about Crooked Horn.

"It seems the arm finally healed but its strength was never the same. The chief couldn't draw a bow or use a lance. Relegated to the role of observer on war parties and buffalo hunts, he spent most of his time directing the growth of the horse herd and trying to breed a strain of animals with great speed and endurance. Yellow Leaf sent the warrior home with an exceptional mare and the message that he held no grudge."

"Held no grudge?" Juan almost shouted. "The man tried to kill Yellow Leaf's son!"

"True, but Yellow Leaf was a wise man. He knew that nursing the warrior back to health and giving him a good horse was a story that would ultimately spread through the Comanche nation. Not only had the ancient legends proved true, but the great power of the people from the canyon was matched by their generosity and goodwill. No Comanche would risk treachery to the family in the future.

"Oh, one other thing," Great Grandfather smiled. "It came to light that on the very night of the horse race the shaman disappeared from the Comanche village."

"Good thing," observed Sophia. "He might not have survived when Crooked Horn recovered."

"Where was Tukor when the wounded Comanche showed up?" asked Juan. "You didn't mention his role in questioning the warrior."

"He was far away. But that's for next week," said the old man with a twinkle in his eye. "I have to call on Mrs. Martinez and you should probably take advantage of this sunny weather. It's supposed to storm again tomorrow."

CHAPTER 23

Return Home

It was agonizing for Tukor to ride. Although Zolin and Ohtli kept the pace to a slow walk, every step of the bay stallion caused the wounded man searing pain. Once out of sight of the lodges, he slumped forward, nearly unconscious, a groan periodically escaping despite his efforts to remain silent. Guided by the stars, they rode through the night to put as much distance as possible between themselves and the village. Zolin had seen the fearsome burn on Crooked Horn's arm, but he had no way of knowing of the chief's now naked fear of his visitors and that pursuit was completely out of the question.

When they stopped at dawn, Tikaani explained to the others that he was experienced in dealing with healing and went to work. As Shadow sat nearby watching, the men lowered Tukor onto a robe spread on the ground. The slave cut off his cotton shirt and ran fingers over the wounded man's chest. He determined which ribs were broken and pressed one that had separated back into place, wringing a moan through the patient's clenched teeth. He then had the two men cut a long strip, a foot wide, from one of the buffalo hides. They carefully lifted Tukor from the robe and held him upright while the slave skillfully wrapped the skin firmly around his torso from hips to chest. From a pouch at his side, Tikaani produced a bone needle and a length of dried gut, with which he secured the wrap. Back on the robe Tukor fell instantly asleep, the great wolf at his side.

During the afternoon the injured man woke briefly. He was fed thick soup by the slave and almost immediately fell back to sleep. There was a faint band of light in the east when he next opened his eyes. He lay still for a few moments, both to think about what had happened and to forestall the pain movement would bring. When he finally sat up, he was pleasantly surprised: the skin firmly wrapped around his waist reduced discomfort to a dull throbbing.

Ohtli and Zolin were loading the packhorses and Tikaani had lit a small fire, over which he was heating soup. Getting gingerly to his feet, Tukor approached the slave.

"You seem to have many skills," he commented, touching the wrap.

"Hunting was dangerous where I grew up," answered Tikaani. "Broken bones were commonplace."

"Where was that?" the younger man asked.

"Far away to the north," said the slave, gesturing with one hand in that direction.

"In the lands of the Great Water?"

"You know of it?" Tikaani's eyes widened in surprise.

"The traders have told us," replied Tukor. "My great, great grandmother tried to go there with her brother when she was young, but on the way they encountered The Beast and stopped."

"The Beast?"

"A huge animal in the forest," explained Tukor. "They said it nearly wiped out an entire hunting party."

"Oh…the great beasts I know all live in the water," said the slave. "But they are capable of killing entire hunting parties as well," he added grimly.

For the next few days they rode slowly across the great plains of the Llano Estacado under sweeping blue skies with not a hint of a cloud. Tall grass stretched to the horizon on all sides, unbroken by rocks, trees, or hills. But for their unerring sense of direction, and the faint trail they'd made coming in, they'd have wandered about completely lost, as had so many before them and as would so many after them.

On the afternoon of the seventh day, they arrived at the settlement outside the hidden box canyon. Here the robes were carefully stored in an adobe warehouse and Zolin and Ohtli reunited with their families. It was nearly evening when Tukor led Tikaani through the great crack in the escarpment to the beautiful valley beyond. Shadow bounded happily about, reacquainting himself with familiar smells. The slave muttered something in a strange tongue as he took in the scene.

"What did you say?" asked Tukor.

"'Had I been a slave here, I would gladly have stayed,'" translated Tikaani, staring at the 200 foot walls tinged red from the setting sun, the lush grass meadows spotted with feeding horses, and the three white houses surrounded by flowers. "The legends are wrong. They tell of it as a dark and dangerous place." The wounded man stared at him.

"When did you hear the legends?"

"After you were attacked and the lances disappeared in flames, ancient stories burned through the village like a wildfire. Tales of great monsters, half-animal, half-human, emerging from smoke and fire out of the sky to devour your enemies. Many people wanted Crooked Horn to send you away that night."

"This piece of silver has protected our family for many generations," said Tukor, pulling the medallion from under his shirt. "I suspect the chief wanted its power for himself."

"Apparently it didn't desire to be parted from you," answered Tikaani dryly, having been filled in by Zolin about the scene at the rock. "I had my own fears," he went on candidly. "I had to move it aside when I wrapped your ribs, but I didn't dare touch it. I used the thong to pull it aside."

"You were wise," said Tukor with a faint smile, "although I don't think it would have harmed you. Danger to the Wearer seems to trigger it." He slid from his horse as his father and mother approached, questioning looks on their faces about his somewhat cocoon-like appearance.

CHAPTER 24

Destiny

IN THE DAYS THAT FOLLOWED, Tukor's grand-mother Ria brought out the ivory carvings acquired by Lita nearly a century earlier and questioned Tikaani closely about his home. He told of lands bordered by endless water, great forests, and fish the length of many horses—just as the traders had described so long before. But there was more. His home was much further north: a land where the sun disappeared and the people lived in near darkness for many moons. It was a place of great cold where people lived in homes made from snow and sometimes couldn't venture out for days because of great storms, a region roamed by large white bears, equally at home on land or in water, fearless hunters of men and animals. But it was also a land of contrast, where the sun never went down for many moons, a place of warmth and great beauty, filled with boundless game and fish.

"How can this be?" Tukor wondered, as he listened to the slave's stories day after day. To one from the desert, they seemed preposterous. Yet, as time went by, a dream began to grow in him to visit these places, to experience the strange and wonderful things Tikaani talked about. Some weeks later he broached the subject as they returned from a sheep hunt.

"How long would it take to reach these lands?" he asked the former slave.

"I don't know," replied Tikaani. "I was captured as a youth when our band was forced south after a severe winter. While I was foraging in the forest one day, some men appeared and caught me. They sold me to a trader who kept me for several years before he sold me to the Navajo. During those years we traveled great distances and I lost track of how far we came."

"What happened to the rest of your people?" asked Tukor.

"I don't know. I never saw anyone from the village again. Perhaps they survived and returned to the north."

"Crooked Horn said the old trader who brought us the message about horses tried to acquire you," said Tukor. "They call him 'One Eye' because he lost his left eye in an accident or a fight. I met him at the pueblo and he looks like he could be one of your people."

"My people aren't traders. We rarely leave the north, except in time of need. He might be from those who live in wood houses at the edge of the Great Water. I never saw him because the old women hid me whenever he came."

"Would you like to go home?" asked Tukor. The slave stopped and stared at him.

"I've thought about nothing else since I was captured. No matter how they beat and tortured me, I never stopped trying to escape. The first trader had to tie my hands and feet every night that I was with him. The Navajo did the same. Only the Comanche left me loose after dark, because they knew I couldn't escape in the grassland and they would have tortured me to death if I had tried."

"Why haven't you left us?"

"I told you the night I came to your lodge. You and the wolf were meant to come for me," replied Slant Eyes with a grin. "We three have a destiny together."

CHAPTER 25
Old Friendships

WHEN TUKOR TOLD THE family he was planning a trip to the far north when the weather warmed, his grandmother was elated.

"It's the same dream Lita had," she declared. "She had many adventures on the quest, although she and her brother never reached the Great Water."

"I know, Grandmother," replied Tukor. "We will follow her path and Tikaani will guide us to the white land beyond."

The old woman loved to sit beside her house in the warm afternoon sun, and during the following days she retold the stories to Tukor and Tikaani that she'd heard about Lita and Rutu.

"Badger Snarling and Beast Blinder are long dead, but I believe their families still live in the valley with the jagged peaks. When you approach, be sure to wear the medallion in plain sight and the Utes will welcome you. For many, many years they kept an empty lodge for our family, as a token of gratitude for the siblings' help when the village was dying. Rutu and Beast Blinder visited Badger Snarling every year until the Crow warrior finally married a Ute girl and moved there permanently. Lita took a young horse to each of their children when they reached three years of age. Now those children have grandchildren," she said with a smile.

The two men listened intently as she passed on Lita's description of strange animals with huge horns and ferocious brown bears in the game paradise below towering gray peaks. Descriptions of warm streams and fountains of water shooting from the earth were met with astonished looks. But about the fortunes of the Crow band she knew nothing.

"If you find them, the elders may have tales about the fight with The Beast. As with the Utes, keep the medallion in sight upon encountering anyone, for the stories of its power may have survived. Failing to meet the Crow, travel to the western valleys and search for people from the far side of the mountains hunting buffalo: it was reported they could guide one across the mountains to a vast river leading to the Great Water."

Tukor turned to his father and pulled the perfectly repaired cougar head skin from a buckskin pouch. The ears had been stuffed with clay and the jaw, with its fearsome teeth, had been sewn into the mouth so the mask had a snarling appearance.

"One of the women in the village made this for me from the cat that attacked our colt," he said. "Something like it was used by our ancestors against their enemies. Please keep it safe until I return." Yellow Leaf nodded in agreement.

CHAPTER 26
Ute Village

So it was, on a warm spring day more than a century after Lita and Rutu had set out, that Tukor and Tikaani departed for the far north. Each rode a powerful buffalo runner and led a second one packed with gear. They stopped briefly at the village in the main canyon for Tukor to say goodbye to several friends, then headed down-valley for the path to the desert floor. Days later they found themselves at one end of a huge valley bordered on the east by a steep mountain range topped with jagged peaks covered in snow. The river they'd been following angled away west, toward foothills ascending to forest-clad mountains. Before them miles and miles of flat grassy terrain stretched north to distant summits. Out in the basin, numerous black dots marked the presence of grazing buffalo.

"This is the valley spoken of by my family," said Tukor as they stopped to take in the striking scene. "We're to follow the river upstream to find the Ute village." But Tikaani was staring at the snowy pinnacles on their right, a big smile on his face.

"Snow," he grinned. "I'd like to climb up there just to feel it!"

"Surely you saw snow when you were with the Comanche," said his companion.

"Yes, but never like that," the former slave pointed up. "That snow is deep, like it is in my land, not just a mere covering that disappears the minute the sun touches it!" As they followed the river westward, Tikaani couldn't resist swiveling around on his horse to stare at the vast snowfields covering the peaks.

An hour later they saw smoke rising from the cottonwoods on the north side of the river and before long a group of nearly 20 riders emerged from the trees and cantered toward them. The oncoming warriors showed no sign of aggression because it was obvious that the two men leading the fully loaded packhorses posed no threat. When they were 100 yards away, Tukor slid the medallion out and let it rest on his white cotton shirt. The exposed silver flashed in the rays of the afternoon sun and the 20 men instantly pulled up. There was a brief consultation and two of them turned and raced back toward the village. With whoops and shouts, the rest covered the remaining 75 yards at dead run, excitedly waving hands over their heads. They pulled to an abrupt stop in a cloud of dust before Tukor and Tikaani, every one of them grinning widely. Two of the men edged their horses forward.

"My great grandfather saw the medallion when he was a very young boy," said one of them, a strikingly powerful man. "He said on his deathbed that one day it would come back to the valley."

"Who was your great grandfather?" asked Tukor.

"He was the son of Beast Blinder and had the name 'Knows No Fear,' in memory of a great warrior in the north.

"Ahhh, Beast Blinder was like a son to my great, great grandmother Lita," replied the New Mexican with a smile. At this, excited murmurs spread among the rest of the riders. Now it was the Ute leader's turn to smile.

"It's said that a woman always appeared with a horse for Knows No Fear and his brothers and sisters when they became three." The other man, slender and wiry, leaned forward to grasp Tukor's right forearm with his.

"Your ancestor and her brother saved the life of my great, great grandfather when he was too weak to hunt for the few survivors of the sickness. After he recovered, he became a renowned leader of our people and kept a lodge always ready for your family. Although many, many years have passed since the last visit, the tradition has been maintained; two of our men have gone to ready it for you.

"Your ancestor must have been Badger Snarling," said Tukor. "Our legends recount that he became a great horse trainer."

"The stories passed down from him say Lita was the best rider he ever saw and he tried to copy her," replied the Ute.

The visitors were stunned at their reception by the village. True to the tradition, a spacious lodge awaited them at the edge of the community. After their horses were unpacked, each was led to water by a young boy and then turned in with a large herd grazing nearby. The boys returned to stand outside the lodge until the two men stepped out.

"Each of us is responsible for one of your horses," said the oldest lad solemnly. "We will be close by and you only need ask which you want and we'll fetch it." Too startled to speak, Tukor could only stare. Tikaani took a step forward.

"We are honored by your kindness. Surely one day you will become great warriors." The four turned away, eyes shining at the compliment. "It would seem these people still hold your family in high regard," the ex-slave exclaimed to Tukor.

A great fire was built in the center of the village and everyone feasted on buffalo, venison, elk, and baked trout. It turned out the two men descended from Beast Blinder and Badger Snarling were co-leaders of the tribe: such was the regard for each family's wisdom and bravery. Owl Swooping had grown up listening to stories of the great battle his ancestor had fought with Lita and Rutu against The Beast. Marmot had been raised knowing the Utes in the Great Valley wouldn't have survived if it had not been for the southerners. Both were overjoyed at Tukor's sudden appearance and did everything possible to make the visitors welcome.

Hours were spent sitting against willow back-rests in the spring sun, surrounded by men, women, and children, telling and retelling stories of battles and hunts and horses. Of course the Utes wanted to examine the buffalo runners and test their own horses' speed against them. The races were highly spirited and attended by everyone, but rarely did the Indians win. Owl Swooping asked Tukor about the sling and the New Mexican obliged with demonstrations that left the people in awe.

"Beast Blinder was well trained in the sling," said Tukor. "At least one of my ancestors would have died otherwise."

"I know," replied the Ute. "But the skill has been lost by our people."

"We use the bow and the atlatl also," answered Tukor. "But the sling has certain advantages of its own," he added dryly. Ten days of feasting, hunting, and riding passed quickly and then it was time to leave. Two days earlier, Owl Swooping had approached Tukor.

"I've always wanted to go north and find the Crow people from whom Beast Blinder came," he said. "Would you accept another rider on your quest?"

"What of your family?" inquired Tukor, knowing the chief had two small children.

"My wife and Marmot's wife are sisters. The family will be well cared for and I'll be back by the snows." Glancing at Tikaani, Tukor saw acceptance in his eyes.

"We'd be honored to have you," he said.

CHAPTER 27

Spring Vacation Plans

"GREAT GRANDFATHER, YOU'RE not going to believe this!" Juan cried as their relative opened the front door on a Saturday morning several weeks later. The twins stepped inside, careful to leave wet footgear on the boot tray inside the door and shrug out of their parkas. The skies had cleared the day before and the temperature had plummeted far below zero during the night, creating a rosy tinge to their cheeks.

"Well, why don't you try me?" the old man grinned.

"We're going to Santa Fe over spring break," the words tumbled out in excitement. "The school has arranged for the entire 8th Grade to spend three days learning about the history of the area and visiting interesting sites. We're going to be walking on the same ground our ancestors did for so long."

"You're right, but don't forget that was three and four hundred years ago—the climate and conditions have changed since then. Santa Fe's now a modern city extending for miles in almost every direction. But, as we've discussed, the Palace of the Governors and the Central Square are still there, and there are many pueblos in the area.

"If you use your imaginations, you might be able to visualize what it was like for Cuto be marched into the Colonel's office for interrogation, then thrown into a storeroom nearby because they had no jail. Now, there are cars and traffic at night, but if you try to shut it out you might recreate the shadow of Marquez as he slipped in to flay Cuto with the whip.

"At the pueblos there'll be lots of vendors and tourists. Try to shut them out and imagine the warriors rising from cover to attack Marquez' command, the deadly rain of arrows, clouds of dust, and the screams of wounded men. It all happened just as I've said, but you have to eliminate the modern distractions to feel it!"

"I can't wait!" exclaimed Sophia. His words had brought back so many images of the family's history that she tingled with the prospect of actually getting to the area where it all happened.

"I stopped over to see Mrs. Martinez on Tuesday," said Great Grandfather, changing the subject. "She seems to think the two of you are some kind of saints! She says she's getting fat! All she has to do is sit around and eat these incredible meals." The twins blushed. "She also says you've saved her life. She'd have given up if the family had moved her to the home in Alamosa." There was silence for a moment.

"What we've done doesn't compare to what you've done for her ever since Mr. Martinez died," said Sophia softly. "You've supplied her with food from your garden all these years and maintained her house. We've just cooked a few meals."

"Well, she seems to think otherwise," replied the old man, handing each of them a package wrapped in brown paper.

"What has she done?" exclaimed Juan as they ripped away the paper. Inside was a pair of knee-high leather moccasins. The rich tan material was wonderfully soft, except for the thick, rough soles; a small fringe at the top hid a thin strap for keeping them tight.

"Normally she'd have decorated them with quills and beads, but she's unable to see well enough now. Most of the work she did by feel. The soles are made to be replaced and the design allows for growing feet. As you break them in they may become the most comfortable footwear you'll ever have and, of course, they can be worn over or under jeans."

"What's the material and how did she get it?" asked Sophia as she pulled the moccasins on.

"It's tanned deerskin and the soles are made from buffalo hide, just like the old days." Great Grandfather grinned, "I have a source."

CHAPTER 28
Close Call

THREE WEEKS AFTER LEAVING the Ute camp, the riders entered the wildlife paradise discovered by Lita and Rutu more than 100 years before. A great valley filled with game of astounding variety, and bisected by a large river, was flanked four or five miles to the west by a stunning array of jagged peaks rising thousands of feet in the air. On the eastern side, tree-covered slopes gave the whole area an enclosed feeling, like a vast bowl. The little group paused for a long time taking in the sight before riding slowly forward.

"It's just as the stories describe," murmured Tukor.

"As magnificent as our valley is at home, it's nothing like this," declared Owl Swooping, spellbound by the sight.

"In all my travels, I've never seen anything like it," said Tikaani.

Two bears rearing out of the grass 20 yards to the right interrupted their reverie. Each stood almost nine-feet-high and was covered with shaggy brown hair. With fearsome roars, they dropped to the ground and charged. The horses needed no encouragement and took off at a dead run, pack animals close behind. After a short chase, the grizzlies stood again and roared their defiance at the retreating horsemen.

"That'll teach us not to forget our surroundings," laughed Owl Swooping. "The bears at home are smaller, though no less aggressive."

"We rarely see them in the desert," said Tukor with awe, "and certainly nothing that big!"

As they rode up the valley they crossed streams flowing to join the river, almost all of them dammed at intervals into large ponds. Tree stumps with pointed tops proliferated around the ponds and several clumps of mud and sticks always poked above the water.

"What's that?" asked Tukor as a distinct "V" moved across the surface of one of the little lakes.

"We call them 'beaver,'" explained Owl Swooping. "They have broad, flat tails which they use to slap the water when danger approaches. There, do you hear it?" A splash clearly sounded along the edge of a pond they were approaching and a small brown animal sank from sight beneath the surface. "Their lodges are those piles of sticks and mud."

"How do they get in?" asked Tikaani, fascinated by the strange water creatures.

"Underwater there are openings and tunnels up into the lodge. Beneath those sticks is a chamber, sometimes big enough to accommodate a person."

"What about the tree stumps?" inquired Tukor. "They all look the same."

"That's because the beaver gnaw through the wood until the tree topples. They can actually make it fall in the direction they want. When it's down, they chew it into pieces to make their dams." Owl Swooping smiled, "They are very busy little animals."

That night they camped along the river and, after staking out the horses nearby, Tukor and Tikaani left the Ute roasting the delicious saddle meat of a mule deer and went down to the water to observe a vast flock of ducks that had settled in a large eddy just offshore.

"There are so many birds!" exclaimed the New Mexican. "We have them in the desert but they are much smaller and not in such numbers."

"It's because of the water," explained the former slave. "Birds like these, and the big white ones with black necks over there on the far bank, come north during the warm season. They hatch their young, teach them to swim and fly, and then go south when the weather changes."

Engrossed in observing the ducks, and deafened by the squawking, the two men never heard the noise in the heavy grass just downstream. A flicker of motion in the corner of his eye caused Tukor to swing around. Looming above him was a massive dark shape over seven feet tall. Huge ears were laid back on a misshapen head with blazing eyes. As enormous split hooves struck out at him, he only had time to shove the slave out of the way before a glancing blow to the side of his head hurled him backward into the river and all went black.

The New Mexican woke to splitting pain in his skull. He was lying beside the fire and the sun was well up in the sky. He felt Shadow's body alongside him and tried to move, but a hand on his shoulder gently held him down.

"Stay still." He recognized Tikaani's voice, but the face above him was blurred and indistinct. "Swallow this." A warm bitter liquid entered his mouth. He complied and immediately drowsiness engulfed him and he knew no more.

The sky was red with dawn the next time Tukor opened his eyes. Again the slave made him lie still, but the pain was decidedly less. Further, he could clearly see the man's features as Tikaani bent over him. He was fed more liquid; however, this time it was thick and delicious. He realized his head was cushioned on a thick pile of grass and he was covered with a warm sleeping robe, Shadow in his usual place pressed against him.

"What happened?" he croaked.

"Tikaani and the wolf saved your life." Owl Swooping's face came into view above him. "There was a cow moose and calf in the tall grass just a few yards from you. Even the wolf never heard the charge because of the ducks, but you must have seen her at the last minute because you shouldered Tikaani out of the way. She knocked you into the river and was going after you when the wolf jumped for her throat. She spun and reared up, narrowly missing his head with her hoofs. Using the distraction, your friend leaped up and buried his knife in her neck. As she turned to attack him, the calf bleated and drew her away. It was over as swiftly as it started, but Shadow and Tikaani's quick action prevented one of those sharp hooves from killing you." The ex-slave's face came into view again.

"You saved my life and we saved yours," he smiled. "I told you the three of us have a destiny together."

"It would appear so," replied Tukor, stroking Shadow. A contented rumble from the big animal seemed to indicate agreement.

CHAPTER 29
Deadly Ponds

For the next couple of days Tukor suffered from headaches and dizziness, but when they moved out on the third day he had recovered. Their progress along the river involved passing through vast herds of buffalo, elk, antelope, and deer. The weather was warm, with an occasional afternoon rainstorm, and before long they left the stunning peaks behind and entered a land of forested hills and mountains. A few days later they topped a rise and beheld the enormous lake Lita had described. It stretched almost out of sight to the north, little whitecaps stirred by the wind running across its surface. Only Tikaani had seen so much water in one place and they sat their horses for many minutes trying to take it all in. Finally Tukor spoke.

"My great, great Grandmother said a river flows from the north end of this lake and falls down a steep canyon before flattening out and running north. Following that river will take us to the land of your ancestors." He stared at Owl Swooping.

"That is the same word I received," replied the powerful Ute. "Perhaps we will find some who remember..."

They found the river and followed it to the rim of an enormous cleft carved by the water. Hundreds of feet below, the water boiled and roared over steep rapids and waterfalls, sending clouds of mist boiling up toward them. As they rode along the rim for several miles, the unleashed fury of the river in the long and precipitous drop was unlike anything they'd ever seen. The horses were frequently reined in, riders captivated by the awesome maelstrom beneath. The legends had not prepared them for this.

Finally the terrain began to level out and the river returned to a more normal pace, gently snaking through forests and out into serene grasslands, always heading north. As they made camp that night, far from the canyon, Owl Swooping pointed out several plumes of white rising from the forest far in the distance to the northwest.

"Perhaps it's smoke from hunting fires," he suggested as they feasted on strips of roasted elk meat and wild onions

"Perhaps," answered Tukor, "although we are many days' ride from the western valleys Lita spoke of."

"Others might have come up-river for the buffalo we see everywhere," commented Tikaani. "I'm surprised we've seen no hunters before this."

In the morning, the plumes were still visible, almost unchanged from the night before. After loading the packhorses, the three headed away from the river toward them, discussing the fact that hunting parties would probably camp close to the river and that the plumes somehow didn't look like wood-smoke. Two hours later they were proved correct. Among the hills they found a wide area of pale ground, completely devoid of vegetation. In it resided several ponds of astonishingly brilliant hues: pale blues, greens, and oranges. Among the ponds were at least four small basins containing bubbling tan mud; every minute or two, one would emit a puff of steam into the air. The rising steam collected and formed the plumes they had seen from afar.

Owl Swooping tried to walk his horse onto the pale ground but it snorted and jumped to the side.

"Something about the stories tells me we should be careful," said Tukor, sliding off his buffalo runner and approaching the strange ground. He kneeled at the edge and held out his hand. "I feel heat," he announced, standing to face the others. "I remember now, there was something about Rutu burning his hand in the mud." As he tried to recall the incident, the long howl of a wolf rang from the forest beyond the clearing, quickly followed by yelps and howls. Shadow answered with a deep growl, hair straight up along his back, but a quiet word from Tukor silenced him as the men backed their horses out of sight into the trees. What followed none could have predicted.

Out of the woods appeared a yearling buffalo calf. It was stumbling as it ran, tongue out, white slobber covering its shoulders. Even at distance the men could see the crazed look in its eyes as it sought to escape the deadly pack coming through the trees behind. It ran across the grass fringe of the open area and straight out onto the pale ground. Trying to skirt the blue pond, it slipped and went down heavily, sliding forward and bawling loudly. By now the wolf pack had emerged from the forest and stood at the edge of the cleared ground, tongues lolling; not one ventured forward. The doomed calf slid right into one of the bubbling basins and immediately began to sink from sight, the stench of burned hair mingling with steam. In less than 20 seconds it was gone, mud bubbling on as if nothing had happened.

The men stared at each other, stunned. One of the wolves caught a flicker of movement from the horses and the pack vanished into the forest.

"I think this explains why we've seen no hunters," observed Tikaani nervously. "It's an area protected by angry spirits. Think of the violence of the water in the canyon: it was like a dark force straining to get out."

"I'm not sure," replied Tukor. "Lita talked of streams where the water was warmed from underground. Both she and Rutu loved it for bathing."

"The ponds are beautiful, but the area is a trap," noted Owl Swooping. "If one is careful, like the wolves, there's no danger." Nevertheless, all three felt a sense of relief as they turned away from the colorful ponds.

CHAPTER 30
Left to Die

Tɪᴋᴀᴀɴɪ ᴡᴀꜱ ᴛʜᴇ ꜰɪʀꜱᴛ ᴛᴏ ꜱᴇᴇ birds circling in the distance, so far away they were only specks in the blue. It was a week later and countless miles separated the riders from the deadly mud pots to the south.

"Vultures," the ex-slave muttered, gesturing at the sky.

"They're still high," observed Owl Swooping. "There might be wolves on a buffalo or elk carcass. They drop lower when the wolves are satisfied." But an hour later the big carrion eaters, now clearly visible, were still circling on thermals a few hundred feet above the ground.

"Maybe it's grizzlies," said Tukor. "It takes more time for them to get filled up." As they drew closer, however, no predators came into view. The vultures seemed to be circling a low hill to their right, several hundred yards away from the river they were following. Tikaani, who had extremely sharp eyes, suddenly drew up.

"That's not a kill. Someone is lying there and the birds are coming to the ground." With that, he leaned forward and urged his horse into a run toward the hill.

The others followed, whistling to the packhorses who obediently picked up the pace and came on behind. As the riders thundered up the little rise, vultures flapped heavily into the air and resumed circling. The sight that met the travelers' eyes was startling.

A naked youth was staked spread-eagled on the ground, unconscious but seemingly unharmed. Two arrows had been shot into the dirt almost touching either side of his chest and two others deep in the soil on each side of his head, so close he couldn't turn it. His long hair had been stretched out in a fan shape on the ground. To the right side of his head, beyond reach, was a small bowl containing a block of pemmican and a deer stomach filled with water. To the left side of his head, at an equal distance, was a small deerskin pouch with the tip of a black feather sticking from it. Quite astonishing was the fact that despite his unmistakable Indian features, the boy's skin was extremely pale and his hair pure white.

Tikaani was off his horse in an instant, cutting the boy's arms and legs free from the stakes and raising his body to a sitting position for Tukor to trickle water into his mouth. Coughing and spluttering, the youth's eyes flew open. He stared at the men in stark terror, until he slowly realized they meant no harm and allowed himself to sink back against Tikaani. He pointed to the water skin and urgently held out his hands. After a long drink, he shut his eyes and instantly fell asleep.

"Let's make camp at the river," said the former slave. "I don't think he's hurt, but I want to examine him." They left the site exactly as they had found it and Tikanni propped the boy in front of him on his horse for the short ride to a cottonwood thicket beside the waterway. Laying him on a robe, the little man gently probed the boy's body until he was satisfied there were no broken bones or internal injuries.

"Whoever it was didn't hurt him," he reported to the others. "But they didn't want him to live either."

"They were frightened," announced Owl Swooping in a low voice. Scared of no man, he had nevertheless kept his distance from the strange looking Indian. "It's the pale skin and white hair. Whoever did this was afraid he was a spirit who would come back to ruin their hunting and strengthen their enemies if they killed him. That's why they left food and water: a peace offering if he freed himself. The arrows were also for his use if he survived."

"His body looks normal enough to me," said Tukor doubtfully. "He is a little thin, but normal. If his hair were cut off, he'd look like any of the boys herding your horses at home, just lighter skinned." But Owl Swooping didn't seem to be convinced and, grabbing his bow, took off through the trees to hunt.

The next morning the boy woke with the men and sat on his robe cross-legged watching them move about checking on the horses and making preparations for the day. His face, framed by his strange looking hair, was impassive—eyes watchful but not afraid. Tikaani squatted down in front of him and handed over a thick piece of venison left over from their evening meal. The youth attacked it ravenously: it was clear he'd not eaten for some time. When the meat was gone, the older man tried to speak with him in a number of dialects but each one drew only a shake of the head. Finally the boy's fingers began to move in the universal language of the plains.

"I cannot hear," he signed. "My hearing disappeared in the sickness that came when I was very young." Tikaani's fingers flew in response.

"Did the sickness also change your hair and skin?"

"My Grandmother says I was a light skinned baby, but the sickness made it worse and turned my hair completely white." After a pause he signed, "I nearly died."

"Where are your people?" asked the former slave.

"They are several days walk north and west of here. I was on a vision quest when the Blackfoot hunters found me."

"You're fortunate they didn't kill you."

"I think they wanted to, because they argued for a long time among themselves before staking me to the ground. When they stood over me with the bows drawn, I thought the arrows were to kill me. They were yelling loudly for me to remember that they'd spared my life and left food and an offering."

"How long were you staked out?"

"I was there for one night while they camped nearby, which probably saved me from predators. They left early yesterday morning. I would have surely died from wolves or coyotes last night if you hadn't come." Owl Swooping had been standing behind Tikaani watching the conversation. The description of the sickness had reassured him that the boy was not a spirit and he leaned forward.

"What do they call you?" his fingers asked.

"What else but 'Snow,'" the boy shrugged.

"Can you ride?" questioned the big Ute.

"Of course, I'm one of the lookouts for our horses." Tukor couldn't help grinning at Swooping Owl.

"I told you he'd be just like one of those boys watching your herd if his hair was cut off," he announced triumphantly.

CHAPTER 31
Yellowstone Park

"WHAT KIND OF DISEASE would do that to a child?" interrupted Sophia, staring at Great Grandfather.

"I wondered about that myself," replied the old man. "One might think of an albino condition, but that doesn't necessarily explain the deafness. I did some research and found out there's a rare condition called 'Waardenburg Syndrome' that can cause pale skin in an infant, an increasing loss of hearing and whitening of the hair. We can't know for sure if that's what Snow had, but it's certainly a possibility.

"Anyone outside of his village would certainly have been superstitious about his appearance. Normally one tribe would have put to death or enslaved a captive from another tribe, but the Blackfoot hunters were clearly conflicted about what to do. Owl Swooping was right: they had decided if he was a spirit he could come back to cause them problems. They erred on the side of caution: stake him out to die on his own, or by natural means. If he was a man they'd eliminated him as custom dictated; however, if he was a spirit he could free himself and they'd curried his favor by leaving food, weapons, and a talisman of good will."

"They probably left the area pretty quickly," observed Juan.

"I'm sure they did," laughed Great Grandfather. "How about another scone?"

"I've already had three," protested Juan, pushing back from the table. "I wish I had your baking skills. I could make tons of money for the class trip at our next school bazaar."

"While we're taking a break," said Sophia, "I wanted to ask about those mud pots. Is that really what they're like in Yellowstone? And what about the colored ponds?"

"As we discussed last year, Yellowstone Park is actually located on and around three calderas. Calderas result from enormous volcanic explosions. For example, in 1815 Mt. Tambora erupted in Indonesia. It's estimated to have thrown the equivalent of 36 miles of cubic rock into the atmosphere, creating global after-effects. The ash hurled into the stratosphere was such that temperatures in parts of North America and Europe dropped drastically, causing 1816 to be called 'the year without a summer.' The consequences to agriculture were devastating. In comparison, the 1980 eruption of Mt. St. Helens is estimated to have produced one quarter of a cubic mile of rock, causing a fine powder of ash to fall hundreds of miles away, but having none of the global impact of Tambora. However, the supervolcano of the first Yellowstone eruption, 2.1 million years ago, is estimated to have produced an estimated 600 cubic miles of rock. It's staggering to contemplate the global consequences of such an event.

"Beneath Yellowstone is a chamber of magma, or molten rock. Obviously, the heat wants to escape and the disturbance to the earth's crust created by the three eruptions provides outlets for some of the gasses and steam to escape. Thus, Yellowstone is home to many thousands of mud pots, fumaroles, paint pots, and a myriad of geysers.

"The mud pots are caused by steam seeping up through the ground and heating basins of groundwater to a muddy, bubbling mass. The colored ponds can be spectacular. Generally the water is very hot, but not boiling, allowing for bacteria and algae to grow, creating wonderful colors.

"Then, of course, there are the geysers. Everyone knows about Old Faithful, but there are many, many more; some even more spectacular than Old Faithful, though quite irregular."

"We should make a trip over there sometime," remarked Juan. "I'd love to see the geysers."

"And the animals," added Sophia.

"You're right," answered Great Grandfather. "Yellowstone Park is an incredible natural zoo. Black bears, grizzlies, buffalo, mountain sheep, elk, coyote, antelope, deer, and now wolves are all on site. The wolves are hard to find, but people come from all over the country with high-powered spotting scopes, set up at dusk in remote areas like the Lamar Valley, and try for a glimpse of them on distant slopes.

"In addition, the Park has a wonderful variety of birds and small mammals. It's really a magnificent area, as evidenced by nearly 2,000,000 visitors every year." He took a sip of coffee. "How are the plans developing for Santa Fe?"

"Great," answered Sophia. "It's only a month until Spring Vacation and 15 kids are already signed up. We'll probably have more by the time we leave."

"I'm glad," replied Great Grandfather. "It's a chance for you to visit an area of great national significance as well as one that our family was closely tied to." He paused and leaned back in his chair. "Now, where was I?"

CHAPTER 32

Teepee Paintings

TWO DAYS LATER THE TRAVELERS approached a large collection of lodges on the banks of a sizable creek. Nearby, a herd of several hundred horses grazed under the watchful eyes of a handful of mounted youths. Small evening cook fires were burning in front of most teepees, causing a light haze of smoke to drift through the greenery of enormous cottonwoods flanking the stream, and children were dashing about in a variety of play. A group of armed riders suddenly materialized in front of the village and raced toward the approaching group, although not with the intensity of an attack. Tukor knew they had seen the three packhorses and determined the newcomers were probably traders.

Snow, mounted behind Tikaani, raised an arm as the riders closed and the men visibly relaxed, slowing their horses to a trot. When they were a few yards away the leader, clad only in breechclout and moccasins, began to sign at Snow. He was as powerfully built as Owl Swooping, with black hair falling far down his back and hawk-like features. Letting his war club dangle from a wrist by its thong, he moved the fingers of both hands in rapid conversation. After a minute or so, he addressed Tukor in a dialect which neither he nor the others understood. At the shake of their heads, he reverted to sign language.

"You're welcome here," he said. "Snow has explained what happened. You saved his life."

"Vultures drew us to him," replied Tukor. "They are the ones that saved his life."

"The lad has always been a dreamer," answered the Indian. "He told us before he left on his vision quest that a vulture had come to him one night and told him it was time to seek a sign."

"It seems the Blackfoot hunters ruined the vulture's instructions," signed Tukor.

"Perhaps, or perhaps the sign had something to do with your party," said the warrior, directing his gaze at Shadow, standing quietly beside Tukor's buffalo runner. He turned his horse toward the village and motioned for them to follow.

As they approached, several of the horse herders exchanged greetings with Snow through raised arms and a small crowd of people gathered at the edge of the lodges, curious about the visitors. When the leader called out an explanation and the people saw Snow mounted behind Tikaani, smiles appeared on many faces.

"It appears the youth is well regarded here," commented Owl Swooping.

"A dreamer is held in high regard by the Navajo and Comanche," answered Tikaani.

"And by my people," nodded the Ute.

The riders wended their way through the teepees, all covered with a variety of painted scenes, and arrived at one larger than any of the others, set near the edge of the stream. The leader slid from his horse as a beautiful woman clad in buckskin emerged from the lodge. They exchanged a few words and she smiled, turning to Snow who had slipped to the ground and was approaching. Their fingers exchanged greetings and both ducked into the dwelling.

"Make your camp along the creek. The boys will look after your horses with ours," signed the warrior, turning back toward the visitors. "Tonight we will feast the safe return of my son." As they made their way to an open spot at the edge of the village, the customary pack of Indian dogs followed them. Shadow paid no attention and the animals kept their distance, not daring to challenge the big wolf. In minutes, the pack dispersed among the lodges to follow less dangerous pursuits.

After the horses were unpacked and turned out with the herd, the three men made their way to the big teepee. It was clear that Snow's father, Swift Arrow, was the leader of this village. Since it was summer, robes had been set on the ground outside, great chunks of meat were roasting over the fire and other dishes were being prepared while they cooked. Soon other people began assembling, until the whole community was present, and the evening passed with joyful eating and dancing. Curious children cautiously approached the black wolf lying quietly beside Tukor but didn't quite dare touch him. After a gesture of encouragement from Tukor, however, they did toss scraps of meat toward the great black head, laughing with delight as each disappeared with a snap of jaws.

The next morning, after checking on their horses, Tukor and Owl Swooping strolled through the lodges studying the mounts staked out by each. Most of the animals were mustangs, slightly smaller than their buffalo runners but wiry and strong, capable of running great distances. As they drew near the teepee housing Snow and his parents, the morning sun highlighted the many scenes covering its surface. Suddenly Owl Swooping stopped in his tracks.

"A beautiful horse," commented Tukor, thinking the Ute was admiring the chief's animal grazing beside the dwelling.

"No...look!" exclaimed the warrior, pointing at the teepee. There, on a faded buffalo skin that was part of the teepee's covering was a faint image of an animal. It was unlike any animal depicted on the other lodges. It had a shaggy body, huge ears, and a long snake of a nose stretched toward a small figure in front of it. Great curved protrusions stretched to either side of the nose. The eye on the side of its faded head still showed red. Most unusual was the human figure portrayed in front of the animal: it held no bow or lance but a sling extended from its outstretched arm!

"The Beast," murmured Tukor, stepping forward to examine the drawing. "It's The Beast and the boy named Chattering Squirrel! And look!" From the top of a tree, drawn to the side of the images, was suspended the figure of a woman with an ornament clearly hanging from her neck!

Within minutes, the excited Tukor, flanked by Owl Swooping and Tikaani, sat facing Swift Arrow, Snow and his mother across the fire-pit outside the lodge. A circle of important community leaders occupied robes ringing the pit; behind them, the entire village had assembled to witness the meeting. On the robe in front of him lay Tukor's sling and the medallion hung outside his shirt. A long wooden pipe was filled, lit, and solemnly passed around the circle. When it returned to Swift Arrow, he put it down. The New Mexican's hands launched into a description of Lita and Rutu's great adventure to the north.

"So our pasts are intertwined," Tukor concluded after many minutes. "The boy, Chattering Squirrel, earned the name 'Beast Blinder' and journeyed south with my ancestors. He became the forefather of Owl Swooping, who has long wanted to reconnect with the Crow from whom he's descended." The man facing him smiled.

"The legends from our ancients tell the same story, but the connection is even greater," he signed. "My father's grandfather was Knows No Fear and Knife in Hand, gesturing toward his wife, is descended from Pretty on Top! This lodge serves to remind us of the past.

"After your relatives departed that summer, Knows No Fear painted the images on his teepee. He directed they be repainted whenever the buffalo skin wore out, to preserve the story of how our people were saved from starvation by the meat of The Beast and to honor the visitors who helped defeat it. His instructions have been faithfully carried out by many generations."

"Do the legends speak of this?" asked Tukor holding out the medallion.

"You didn't notice?" questioned Swift Arrow. "The teepee skin next to the one with The Beast records many battles the Crow from this village have fought. You will find there the attack on Lita and Rutu. Every generation has heard the story of what the silver did to the arrow aimed at her heart. Every generation has been told that if the pendant with the square hole reappears, it will be worn by a friend of our people." Now it was Tukor's turn to smile.

"The vultures guided us to you."

"Yes," signed Swift Arrow. "But your appearance was foretold years ago. As I mentioned, Snow is a dreamer and our people marvel at his visions. When he was five, he ran to Knife in Hand one morning in great excitement. He had dreamed of a large black wolf lying peacefully in the village, being fed by children."

CHAPTER 33

Nez Perce

AFTER A WEEK OF WARM hospitality, Swift Arrow and a few warriors escorted the three travelers west. They searched great valleys, bordered on each side with high, forested mountains until they found the buffalo hunters. The Crow had good relations with these people, having traded many times in the past for the colorful shells and beads they always carried.

"They call themselves 'Nez Perce,'" Swift Arrow explained. "If we help with their hunt, they'll take you with them over the mountains." With the added skill of the additional riders and their buffalo runners, the Nez Perce quickly acquired and dried all the buffalo meat their packhorses could carry. Before long it was time to start home.

"The lodge will be waiting when you return to our village," Owl Swooping promised as the little group split in half. The Ute had accomplished his objective of finding his kin and desired to travel no further. He would spend the rest of the summer with Swift Arrow and the Crow before heading back to his home in the south.

"Tell Marmot I'll bring him one of the white carvings we talked about," Tukor replied, exchanging a forearm clasp as the horses turned away.

During the hunt, Tikaani had discovered he could understand parts of the Nez Perce language and began to converse haltingly with them. As days went by, the conversations became smoother and a comfortable relationship was soon established. He explained to his companions that the dialect was closely related to his native language.

"I haven't said the words of my people for years," he said. "But many of the Nez Perce words are so similar I can understand them. It must be because we're all from the north."

The party crossed massive mountains on a well-defined trail and several days later arrived at the hunter's village in the western foothills. A great feast was held to celebrate the men's success. A few days later, in return for brightly colored Pueblo blankets, two men agreed to continue on and guide the strangers west toward the Great Water. Their route followed a series of rivers flowing through pleasant, open country and Tukor spent hours signing with the men about the Nez Perce horses. Never had he seen anything like their coloring. Some were white, with brown or black spots, others of solid color interspersed with white spots. Still others were uniformly colored except for white or spotted rumps; there seemed to be an infinite variety of markings. The animals were larger than the plains' mustangs, leggy and powerful, more like horses Tukor trained at home. He learned that the Nez Perce breeding practices were similar to those of his family: aimed at producing the finest horses possible.

From time to time they stayed in Nez Perce settlements located beside steep, tumbling rapids. At such villages, curious wooden platforms extended a few yards over the raging water, as though a flimsy bridge had been started and abandoned.

"Why do they build a bridge and stop?" Tukor wanted to know. Tikaani laughed.

"Those aren't bridges; they're fishing platforms." The New Mexican stared quizzically at the raging rapids.

"If you shoot an arrow or throw a spear, it will surely be lost in that water," he said doubtfully. The former slave nodded.

"They don't use arrows or spears; they use big nets."

"Nets?"

"Yes, strands of fiber woven loosely together like a deep bowl and attached to a long handle." Tikaani made a big circle with his arms and then held them wide apart to indicate the depth.

"I have to see these nets!" exclaimed the New Mexican.

The next time they stopped for the night at a fishing village, Tikaani went to find a fisherman. He returned with a man carrying a five-foot pole on the end of which hung a deep net with a circular opening more than three feet wide. The man handed it to Tukor. Hefting it, Tukor eyed the swiftly moving water boiling over the rocks.

"This would be torn from my grasp the instant I put it in the water," he observed.

"Yes, but he doesn't thrust it into the water," replied his friend. "He catches the fish with when they jump in the air." Tukor stared at him in confusion.

"They jump?"

"Yes. They go up the river to lay eggs. When they reach a steep rapid like this one, they jump into the air to clear rocks and underwater obstructions; that's when these men net them." Thinking of the trout he'd seen speared by the Utes, Tukor studied the net.

"Wouldn't the fish slip through the holes in the net?" Now it was the fisherman's turn to smile as

Tikaani translated. He held his hands wide apart to demonstrate the size of the fish. Tukor's eyes widened.

"That big? I need to see this!" Both men shook their heads.

"It's still summer," explained Tikaani. "The salmon come when the leaves start to turn. But you'll see them," he promised.

"They're called 'salmon,'" Tukor mused at the unfamiliar word.

"Yes. Every year they come from far out in the Great Water up the rivers to the headwaters. Once there, they lay eggs and die."

"Are there enough to feed all these villages?" Both men grinned.

"More than the stars. They feed the villages, the bears, and any other animal that can catch them or feast on the dead bodies."

CHAPTER 34
The Lolo Trail

Due to sports commitments, all of which Great Grandfather attended, two Saturdays slipped by before the twins knocked on his door again. When it opened, their nostrils were enticed by wonderful smells and they knew he had made huevos rancheros for them.

"I hope you didn't have anything to eat," said the old man as they shrugged out of coats and kicked off their boots.

"Not a bite, after we got your message from Mom," laughed Juan. "We know better than to chow down before one of your breakfasts!"

Settled at the kitchen table, talk during the meal centered on the basketball and volleyball tournaments of the preceding weekends. Each twin captained their respective teams and had led them to outstanding records. Sophia was already practicing with the Center High volleyball team after Junior High practices, and the basketball coach for the High School had penciled Juan in as a starting point guard for the following winter. Great Grandfather marveled as he filled their coffee cups. Not long ago it had been cookies and hot chocolate; in a few months they'd be in High School. Sophia was already beautiful, with long black hair, almond-shaped eyes, and flashing white teeth. Juan was as tall as the old man now, handsome and lean, possessed of great strength and balance. Great Grandfather's eyes shone with pride as he settled in his chair.

"I've been looking at a Montana map," said Sophia. "Where do you suppose Tukor met the Nez Perce?"

"It was probably in one of the big valleys on the eastern side of the Bitterroot Mountains," said Great Grandfather. "I believe he and Tikaani were taken across the Bitterroots on what we call the Lolo Trail, down to the Weippe Prairie in Idaho. The Nez Perce used the Lolo Trail for countless generations to cross those mountains. In 1877 it was the route taken by Chief Joseph to escape the U.S. Army on his historic attempt to lead a remnant of his people to Canada."

"Wasn't it also the route taken by the Lewis and Clark Expedition on their way to the Pacific?" asked Sophia.

"Yes. They ran into bad weather in September and nearly didn't survive the crossing," answered the old man. "It seems our hunters went over during the summer."

"What about the Nez Perce horses?" said Juan. "Their coloring sounds like Appaloosas."

"You're right. The Nez Perce are responsible for developing the breed from horses they acquired in the early 1700's. Like the Comanche, they became excellent breeders, gelding animals they considered unsuitable or trading them away. It was the same pattern that Cuto and Ria developed in the canyon to produce superior animals. Today the Appaloosa is extremely popular throughout our country."

"Did the Indians really net salmon as they jumped in the air?" Sophia wanted to know.

"Absolutely!" Great Grandfather exclaimed. "The salmon run in those rivers today is amazing, but nearly two hundred years ago it would have been absolutely unbelievable. Millions upon millions of fish headed to the headwaters of the exact stream they hatched in. There would have been so many jumping up the rapids that a hundred men at every platform would have made no difference. It was a bonanza of food for the people on those rivers."

"Which rivers are we talking about?" asked Sophia.

"Probably the Clearwater, which meets the Snake, which in turn flows to the Columbia River," replied her relative. "That would be their path to the Pacific."

CHAPTER 35

The River

AFTER FOLLOWING THE RIVER for days, the horse-men were forced to ascend the hills beside it for several days because the flow entered an impenetrable gorge. Late one afternoon they topped a ridge and gazed down upon an immense valley stretching to the west. Far below water emerged from the gorge in a smooth ribbon, highlighted by the setting sun, to join a vast river more than half a mile wide. The great blue-gray expanse, above which circled and swooped hundreds of white specks, stretched away through a patchwork of forests and parklands toward the reddening horizon. Tukor was dumbfounded.

"Is that the Great Water?" he signed.

"No," exclaimed one of the hunters, a man named Otter, but it will take you there." Tikaani's eyes gleamed with excitement.

"Yes," he said, "it will carry us there!" The New Mexican glanced at him expectantly, but the man from the north just stared down at the river, a wide smile on his face.

That night they camped just outside the gorge and the next day approached a sizeable village at the junction between the two rivers. Here the Nez Perce were clearly fishermen as well as hunters. The usual horse herd was maintained in wonderful pastureland away from the river and there were numerous log canoes drawn up on the bank. The customary drying racks were everywhere and Tukor observed that many of them held the white and pink flesh of fish while others displayed the red meat of game animals he was used to seeing. Shortly after their arrival, Tikaani and a group of the men walked away toward the riverbank, leaving Tukor and the Nez Perce to unload the packhorses and make camp.

"He's going with them to negotiate the next 'horse' for you," signed Otter with a grin. Tukor had a glimmer of insight but busied himself with getting the gear unpacked so he could get to the river's edge himself. As soon as the horses were turned loose, he set off through the village, a group of children following him and the wolf at a safe distance.

Little waves ran up on the gravelly beach as the New Mexican stared spellbound across the water. The breeze carried a distinct smell of moisture and freshness that he found pleasing. Overhead myriads of seagulls split the air with raucous cries as they searched for food. Even Shadow was intrigued, trotting up and down the shore sniffing at rocks and debris cast up by the river.

A tug on his shirt caused Tukor to swing around. Behind him stood a boy about six years old, holding out a wooden shaft as long as he was tall, the end of which had been carved to a sharp point, one side flared out like half an arrowhead. The boy motioned toward the river and said something. Tukor smiled and shook his head, whereupon the boy walked a short way downstream beckoning for him to follow. A slight indentation of the bank had formed a pool about ten feet long and three feet deep. Into the pool the boy waded, then stood stock still, right hand raised, with the tip of his spear just above the surface of the water.

Tukor stood quietly a few feet away, watching to see what would happen. As his eyes grew accustomed to the water he began to see fish, apparently disturbed when the boy entered the pool, come back to the little basin and position themselves just inside the river's current. Occasionally one would move laterally into the faster water, a white flash showing as it opened its mouth to snatch a bit of food, and then slide back to the quiet water.

The boy remained absolutely motionless for many minutes, until a large fish moved to the upstream edge of the pool, its size clearly dictating possession of the best feeding spot. It slipped out into the current for a morsel and as it returned to its waiting spot, the spear flashed into the water. An instant later the boy, with a broad smile, raised a squirming 20" rainbow trout on the end of the spear. He waded out of the pool, gulls shrieking and diving over his head, and tipped the shaft toward the half-crouched wolf staring intently at the struggling fish. One snap of the jaws, a tug, and Shadow trotted a few yards up the beach to devour his meal.

All the kids watched as Tukor pulled off moccasins and waded out for a try. He copied the boy's actions and found the fish moving back into the pool after he had stood quietly for a few minutes. Again, a large one took the choice spot just beside him, but when he drove the spear down nothing was there. After two more attempts, he looked questioningly at the boy. The youngster stepped into the pool beside him and took the spear. Everything happened as before and soon there was another trout on the end of the spear. The fish was tossed to Shadow, by now finished with the first one, and Tukor took the spear...boy at his side. Once again he tried to copy everything the youth had done and once again came up empty-handed. The boy grinned and grabbed the man's throwing arm, bending it slightly outward so the point of the spear was aimed toward the water at an angle. This time, when Tukor finally drove the shaft down he felt it connect solidly with the body of the trout. He proudly lifted his prize toward the watching group of kids and was rewarded by yells of approval.

"I didn't know the fish aren't under the water where they seem," he explained to Tikaani and the others that night. "They're slightly to one side." The three men nodded gravely.

"It's a lesson we all had to learn as children," signed Otter.

CHAPTER 36

Canoe

ANXIOUS TO RETURN HOME, the two Nez Perce hunters gathered Tukor's four horses and rode away the next morning, promising to care for and keep them for his return in the spring. Tikaani had traded three large gourds and two colorful Pueblo blankets for a 12-foot wooden canoe. Excited about the next leg of the journey, he was forced to wait until midday because his companion was busy giving sling instruction to the children.

They had come to find him for another fishing expedition when a flight of ducks passed overhead on its way down-river. Tukor pointed at the birds and signed whether the kids liked to eat them. Upon receiving an enthusiastic affirmation, he unwrapped the sling and picked up a few small rocks from the beach.

With the fascinated kids gathered around him, he stood at the water's edge, facing inland. Soon, one of the kids pointed to another flock speeding downstream. As the birds approached, the New Mexican started whirling the sling. Sure enough, a few birds at the edge of the flock were over dry land and, as if by magic, one plummeted to the ground as the flock whirred by. Now it was the kids' turn to be amazed and they crowded around, signing for another demonstration. When it was repeated twice more, they began clamoring for him to teach them. In short order he had taught them how to make a sling and they had spread out along the beach to practice, only to be driven away by angry shouts from villagers hit by errant missiles.

"I think it's time we left," laughed Tikaani. "Before you cause any more problems." He led Tukor to where the canoe, already loaded, was pulled up on the gravelly beach.

The craft was dark brown in color, made from a single log first hollowed by fire and then carved with adzes until the sides and bottom were quite thin. Both bow and stern were squared off so it had an ungainly look that belied its maneuverability. The former slave had taken it out into the river before making the trade and found it to be exactly what he wanted. Now, Tukor looked at it closely for the first time.

"You want to take us onto the water in this thing?" he asked with a frown.

"Yes, unless you want to walk for several moons to reach the Great Water. This canoe will carry us there in half of one moon."

"Do you know how to make it go?"

"I grew up on the Great Water," Tikaani smiled reassuringly. "We used boats called 'kayaks,' which are half this size, to hunt fish. We also used large boats, much bigger than this one, to hunt the huge animals that live in the water. I am no stranger to this craft just as you are no stranger to horses.

"I will be in the back, guiding the canoe and teaching you what to do in the front." He handed his friend a wooden paddle with a long narrow blade and demonstrated how it was to be used. "The water is gentle in this valley and you will learn quickly."

Their packs were centered in the middle of the boat, with bows, quivers, atlatls, and spears lashed securely on top for easy access. There was space at the back, behind the gear, and a larger space in front toward the bow.

"What about Shadow?" asked Tukor.

"He will ride behind you in the front," Tikaani gestured toward the bow.

But when the canoe was pulled into the water parallel to the beach, the black wolf wanted no part of it. He crouched low to the ground, head down, and no amount of coaxing could move him. Tukor knelt beside him for many minutes, talking in a low voice and stroking his back, but the big animal wouldn't move. Only a soft whine escaped his throat as he stared up at his lifelong companion. Finally, the man stood up.

"We will go along the edge of the river?" he asked. Upon receiving a nod from Tikaani, he declared, "He will follow us on the ground and, in time, will join us in the boat." Sure enough, as the canoe caught the current and began to move downriver, the black wolf watched for a moment before loping along the bank beside it.

At the start, Tikaani had the New Mexican kneel quietly in the bow with the paddle laid in front of him across the canoe. In this way the man from the desert became accustomed to the movement of the boat. He quickly learned it was tippy and to keep his weight centered.

"It's not unlike keeping balanced on a horse," he thought to himself.

After a short time, Tikaani directed him to begin using the paddle, first on one side and then the other, but when he leaned sideways to put the blade in the water, it caused the canoe to tip dangerously. Fortunately, his companion anticipated the move and countered it from the stern. The craft was narrow and Tukor quickly found he could use the paddle on either side without leaning and as the afternoon progressed he became more and more comfortable with the process. Whenever he glanced back, Tikaani had a big smile on his face—it was clear the ex-slave was extremely happy to be back on the water.

When they pulled in for the night, they had covered many miles. Shadow was waiting for them on the bank, tongue lolling out. He trotted up to Tukor for a quick smell, receiving several strokes on the head in the process, before flopping down exhausted to sleep. He only stirred to devour a large piece of elk meat tossed his way later in the evening. The next morning they were up at daybreak and preparing to leave when Tukor had an idea.

"Leave the canoe pulled up on the bank," he said. "Let me see if Shadow will get in it on dry ground." Tikaani nodded and stepped back. The New Mexican walked to the boat and tossed another big hunk of meat into it up front. The wolf walked over and looked into the boat. The meat was beyond his reach and he turned his head toward Tukor as if inquiring what to do.

"Go on," said the man gesturing at the meat. The animal paused a moment before lightly jumping into the canoe and grabbing the meat. In a flash Tukor was beside the boat, hand on the animal's shoulder to prevent him from jumping out. Momentarily distracted by the meat, the wolf put one paw on it to tear off a piece; in the next moment the men had shoved the canoe into the river and were under way. By agreement, Tikaani handled the boat while his companion, facing backward, quieted Shadow with another big chunk of meat. By the time the wolf had finished eating, the paddler had them well out in the current, over 100 yards from shore. The animal sat staring over the water for a long time while Tukor talked in a soft voice and stroked his neck; all at once he curled up in the narrow confines of the canoe and went to sleep.

CHAPTER 37
The Plaza

"Great Grandfather? Can you hear me?" Sophia's voice came through the cell phone loud and clear.

"Yes, Sophia, I can hear you just fine. Did you get there all right?"

"We arrived last night. In the end only 10 kids were able to make it, but it was a great trip down through Espanola; Mr. Ramos drove the school van and gave incredible descriptions of New Mexican history the whole way. He was better than a tour guide."

"What did you do today?" the old man wanted to know.

"That's what I called to tell you. Our hotel is near the Plaza, so after breakfast Mr. Ramos took us to see the Palace of the Governors. The museum was really neat and when we came back outside the kids wanted to check out all the vendors selling jewelry on the sidewalk. Juan and I asked permission to go across the street to the little park in the middle of the Plaza; we wanted to try to imagine what it was like in 1610 when Lt. Marquez decided to cut off Cuto's nose and ears before blinding and killing him.

"It was the amazing! Standing there with my eyes closed, all the sounds seemed to go away and in my mind's eye I could smell the dust and see the square surrounded by adobe buildings. I saw this man walking slowly across the dirt holding a sword, the sun glinting off its blade; the look on his face was so menacing I couldn't stand it and opened my eyes. Naturally, there was the Plaza with its parked cars, flowers, and shops.

"I turned to Juan and, by the look on his face, knew he'd experienced something similar. He described exactly the same scene I'd imagined; it was so real that his hands started sweating. When he opened his eyes he realized the medallion was warm!

"How is it possible Great Grandfather? That was nearly 400 years ago; yet with our eyes closed it was like we were actually standing beside Cuto. I swear to you I saw a fly in the scene and heard it buzzing!" There was silence for a minute before her relative answered.

"I don't know, Sophia, but it must have something to do with your being Wearers of the medallion. I told you long ago that you are both Wearers, despite Juan being older by 45 seconds; you each see into the past during the Solstices and the silver piece has protected the two of you several times already. How or why this experience was made so real is beyond understanding."

"That's sort of what we thought," replied the girl. "The whole thing is tied to the medallion somehow."

"What are your plans for the rest of the day?"

"Mr. Ramos wants us to see the Loretto Chapel and the outdoor opera house this afternoon. Then we're going to eat at a place he says has great sopapillas. Tomorrow we visit a couple of pueblos and the last day we going to hit museums covering the Santa Fe Trail."

"I saw on the news that three guys escaped from the State Penitentiary down there," commented Great Grandfather. "Have you heard anything?"

"Yeah, it was on the TV this morning. The prison is south of here; but don't worry, the police have them surrounded at a gas station on the road to Albuquerque."

"Good. Well, have a great day tomorrow; I'll be interested to hear if you have any more experiences with the past." After he hung up, the old man sat for a long time staring at the Sangre de Cristo Mountains through his living room window.

In Santa Fe, Sophia became captivated by the Loretto Chapel and barely mentioned the phone call to her brother. The story of the mysterious stranger, who appeared to make the wonderful circular stair after the builders omitted access to the choir loft, was fascinating to the students. They spent so much time studying the details of its construction that Mr. Ramos was hard-pressed to get them out to the Opera House before closing time. Then they persuaded him to let them swim in the hotel's heated pool before supper. After a huge meal, followed by many sopapillas, the group was ready for bed.

The kids were debating a quick visit to the swimming pool the next morning when Mr. Ramos appeared at the breakfast room in a state of excitement. He'd been on the phone with an old friend, an archeology professor at the University of New Mexico in Albuquerque, who had invited them to visit a remote site he was working on at a private ranch 40 miles south of Santa Fe.

"He says it's ancient Anasazi ruins and no one but he and his students have been allowed to see it. He grew up with the rancher's son and finally convinced him it was a site worth serious study. He's offered to take us tomorrow!"

"What about the museums," asked one of the students.

"You can visit the museums at any time," replied Mr. Ramos. "This is the opportunity of a lifetime to see ruins before the general public!" Swept up in their teacher's enthusiasm, the group voiced its wholehearted support.

CHAPTER 38
Hacienda

Sophia STARED OUT THE window at grazing cattle as the van followed a pickup along a narrow dirt road on the Rodriguez ranch. Yesterday's visit to the pueblos had been disappointing because no matter how hard she and Juan concentrated, no vivid scene from the past had come into their imaginations as it had in the Plaza. It had been fun to see the buildings portrayed as they had existed in the past, but they were clearly the product of modern materials and tools. She wondered why their mysterious experience had been limited to the Plaza.

They had left the hotel early to meet Mr. Ramos' friend, Thomas, at a gas station a few miles down the highway toward Albuquerque. From there they had driven south on a county road for nearly an hour to reach the ranch; nearly all the kids had gone to sleep, but Sophia was fascinated by the desert landscape. She tried to imagine her ancestors riding through desolate hills like the ones they were passing; it must have been brutal in the summer heat.

A pair of huge poles on either side of a cattle guard, connected on top by an equally large log, marked the turnoff to the ranch headquarters. The rumble of the van across the cattle guard woke the kids and eyes were rubbed as they began to take in their surroundings. The road wound through a series of low, dry hills for more than a mile to emerge into a stunning setting.

Before them was a large two-story adobe house built in a square around a courtyard. It was old and magnificent: the adobe cream colored, the roof made of red tile, with dark wood shutters flanking every window. Colorful flower-boxes adorned the openings and a generous fringe of green grass encircled the building to merge with enormous cottonwood trees scattered to the sides. Running behind the structure was a large stream, over which a wide bridge led to numerous corrals, outbuildings, and two large white barns.

The van pulled up to a tiled walkway running through a large arched opening in the first floor to the courtyard where the astonished students could see at least two fountains among many flowerbeds. Thomas and Mr. Ramos jumped out just as a tall cowboy in faded jeans and a large stained hat emerged from the courtyard. He shook Thomas' hand warmly and was introduced to Mr. Ramos.

"That must be the rancher's son," observed Juan. "What a place they've got here! No wonder they don't want the public traipsing around." Just then the cowboy strode to the van, pulled open the big sliding door and leaned inside. His lean face had piercing gray eyes above a slightly hooked nose.

"Hey kids, I hear you're from the San Luis Valley."

"Yes, sir," answered Juan, the first to find his voice.

"My family has some great friends up there. When I heard that you and Mr. Ramos were visiting Santa Fe, I thought you should come out and see our ruins. We don't let the public in at the moment, but anyone from the San Luis Valley is welcome. One of my ranch-hands will go with you; he's working on a well for me so we can run cattle up there. It's pretty dry, as you'll see. Be patient: it's a long way but worth it in the end."

"Thank you so much sir, we really appreciate it," replied Juan as a pickup crossed the bridge from the barns behind the house and approached.

After driving for an hour, Sophia finally checked her watch, astounded at how far they had come. In the beginning they had passed a number of fields irrigated by center pivots. These long sprinkler arms, circling a well at a snail's pace, were completely familiar: farmers in the Valley used them extensively. They soon left the pivots and began to travel through pasturelands sprinkled with cattle, but some miles from headquarters the terrain grew noticeably dryer and the cattle scarcer.

Now they were approaching what appeared to be a vast mesa stretching to both sides as far as the eye could see. Rocky hillsides ascended several hundred feet into the air before appearing to flatten on top. Directly in front of them was a large opening in the mesa through which the road continued.

"Don't worry; it's only a few more miles," said Thomas, glancing back at the students.

"I'm glad the van's air conditioned," replied Juan. "That pickup creates a lot of dust! How big is this ranch anyway?"

"It's about 300,000 acres," said the archeologist with a grin. "But a lot of it's pure desert. And by the way, once we enter this gap your cell phones won't work any more." Many of the students had been passing the time with their phones.

"I'm amazed they've worked until now," said Carlos.

"Mr. Rodriguez is pretty progressive," said Thomas. "He shared in the cost of a couple of cell towers so he could have quick communication with employees working away from headquarters, but this canyon is too deep and twisting for the signal to get through."

CHAPTER 39

Ruins

THE LANDSCAPE THE VAN now entered was barren: scarcely a bush or tree broke the vista of rock and dirt. The road turned into a two-wheeled track heading straight along what had become a wide valley between steep hills. Looking at the terrain, Sophia wondered how the Anasazi had managed to survive here. The canyon Cuto and Ria had found had been well supplied with water; in fact, Great Grandfather told them the streams never dried up during the 300 years the family had lived there. Yet she knew the Anasazi had developed clever ways to catch and store rainwater. Thomas would probably tell them how it had been done. All at once the pickup stopped and the ranch-hand waved the van alongside.

"This is where I'm trying to develop a well," he said, pointing to a backhoe and a collection of material beside the track. "You're on your own while I work. Don't make any wrong turns," he grinned at Thomas.

"If we get lost, you'll know where to find us," joked the professor, knowing there was only one track to follow. Ten minutes later, the valley angled to the right and 1,000 yards ahead a sheer wall blocked the way.

"We're here!" exclaimed Thomas, jumping out. The kids looked at one another blankly; there was nothing in sight. Thomas yanked open the sliding door. "Come and see!" As they tumbled from the vehicle, each stopped in awe at the spectacle revealed above them. To their right and 100 feet up a sheer rock face, was an enormous shallow cave containing an ancient cliff house! Hidden from sight by the roof of the van until they got out, it towered over them like a small multi-level city with door and window openings everywhere. Juan and Sophia stared at each other.

"You never said it was a cliff house," murmured Sophia.

"I know," replied Thomas with a serious look. "We deliberately use the word 'ruins.' If the word got out about the well-preserved quality of this dwelling, looters would find ways to get in and desecrate it. Mr. Rodriguez is working on getting it designated as a national historic site, but that takes time so we're being very cautious. Frankly, I'm amazed he agreed to let you see it; I have only been allowed to bring one or two of my most trusted students to survey it. He must have very good friends in the San Luis Valley."

"How do you get up there?" asked Carlos.

"We have extension ladders hidden nearby," explained Thomas, "specially designed for accessing high places."

"How do you get up and down those levels?" someone inquired.

"Good question," said the professor. "The ancients used wooden ladders to reach them. We've managed to carry a couple of extremely lightweight ladders up there. All we're doing is mapping the building until it's protected. It's remarkably well preserved and will hardly need any restoration before being opened to the public.

"They certainly couldn't have been attacked from above," said one of the students, staring at 100 feet of cliff overhanging the cave.

"No, not to mention protection from sun and occasional rain; we think they farmed down here on the valley floor. The desert above is pretty inhospitable."

"Would it be alright to walk around a bit?" asked Juan, glancing at Sophia.

"Of course," replied Thomas. "You all need to work the kinks out for the ride back to Santa Fe."

The twins left the others and strolled casually along the base of the cliff.

"There they are," said Juan quietly nodding at the rock face. "Just as Great Grandfather described." A series of shallow indentations, hardly discernible anymore due to extensive weathering, ascended the cliff toward the cave.

"There are more of them over here," added Sophia. "Surely Thomas knows about them, but he probably doesn't want one of us to try climbing. Do you think it's really the same cliff-house Swallow showed Cuto and Ria?"

"I think it absolutely is," replied her brother. "But there's one way to be certain. Come on." He walked well away from the cliff, opposite the left side of the cave. Cupping hands at the sides of his eyes, Juan focused on the steep rock wall above the cave. "There they are," he said with satisfaction after a minute or so. "Look to the left of the cave and you can see the footholds coming down the cliff to a little ledge accessing the dwelling."

"I see them," said Sophia excitedly, "and the angle of rock at the top isn't quite vertical, so Swallow could have disappeared from sight when she reached the steep part."

"This means the hidden canyon is somewhere behind us," announced Juan. "I wonder if they've found it."

"I'm not sure we should say anything," Sophia responded. "Mr. Rodriguez is trying so hard to keep this quiet until he gets the historic designation."

"Let's keep our eyes peeled anyway as we go back," suggested Juan.

When they reached the well site, Mike was on the backhoe digging a hole. The professor had Mr. Ramos stop the van to show them something else.

"The reason they're digging here is because there are remnants of what appear to be gardens and an outlying community," he explained. "If that's correct, they must have had water. We think the Anasazi may have developed a farming site here to supply the population of the cliff house." Not 100 yards from where Mike was working, a few weather-beaten rocks outlined a series of squares in the ground; nearby some sections of broken adobe poked up from the soil.

Juan and Sophia looked at one another. This was no Anasazi ruin; this was the remains of a village started by Aztecs coming to join Cuto and Ria in their new life! But where were the cottonwood groves and creek Great Grandfather had described? There was nothing but dirt and a few sprigs of sagebrush on the ground. And where was the entrance to the hidden canyon? Simultaneously both of them stared at the western wall of the canyon. It appeared smooth, but a pile of rock and rubble almost 20 feet high had fallen along the side of the cliff directly across from where they stood.

"Do we have time to do some exploring?" Sophia asked the professor.

"Sure, perhaps you'll find something we missed," he replied. With that, the twins headed for the pile of rubble. Halfway there, Juan noticed a cloud of dust down the canyon.

"Someone's coming," he observed.

"It's probably one of the ranch-hands to help Mike," said Sophia. Her brother suddenly stopped, confusion on his face.

"I'm not sure about that," he cried. "The medallion's warm and getting hotter every second!"

CHAPTER 40
Shot At

At Juan's urging, they sprinted to the pile of rubble and ducked behind several large boulders located to one side. Space between the rocks gave them a clear view of the van and backhoe. As they watched the approaching vehicle, Juan glanced around. The boulders hiding them were uniformly sized at about five feet high and offered cover on three sides, open only to the cliff behind. Further, the openings between the rocks gave them clear views of the canyon floor.

"Sophia," he whispered, this has to be the lookout Cuto designed. See how the boulders are arranged? And look behind you!" There, parallel to the cliff, was a crack, 30 feet wide, extending 200 feet up to the rim.

It was angled in such a way as to be invisible from out on the canyon floor.

"It's the entrance to the secret canyon," she murmured in awe.

Just then a pickup, identical to the one Mike drove, pulled up next to the van in a cloud of dust and three men got out. One headed toward the backhoe, gesturing at the ranch hand, and two walked toward Thomas and the school group still poking around the ruins. As Mike switched off the engine, the twins could hear the men shouting at the kids and waving for them to come to the van.

"They've got guns," said Sophia in a horrified whisper. Indeed, each of the men brandished a pistol and had a rifle across his back. A sudden insight gripped Sophia. "It's the convicts. They must have escaped from the gas station"

As they watched, the kids and adults were made to sit on the ground beside the van and one of the men seemed to be engaged in a conversation with Mike. He pointed up the canyon, but the cowboy's hat shook back and forth and he pointed down the valley. It looked like this enraged the man because he leaned down and shouted into Mike's face, but the ranch hand still shook his head.

"I think he's asking Mike if there's an exit to the desert floor up-canyon," guessed Juan. Just then a shriek caused them to pivot back toward the viewing space. One of the men had pulled Rita upright and was holding a pistol to her head! Juan never hesitated. Telling Sophia to follow, he pulled himself to the top of a boulder and yelled at the top of his lungs.

"Leave her alone, you idiot!" Without waiting to see the result, he scrambled up the pile of rubble behind his sister and slid out of sight. A boom sounded and there was a zinging noise off the cliff.

"They shot at us!" yelled Sophia in disbelief.

"Yeah, and at least one of them's probably coming. Run!" cried Juan. It was like the experience they'd had in the Plaza except this was real, not imagined. The sandy floor of the crack, the tiny slice of blue far above, the approaching rock wall with the remains of a gate hanging from a narrow opening in the middle: it was exactly what Great Grandfather had described. After passing through the remains of a wall and second gate, they raced out into a valley bordered by towering ramparts. The broken down ruins of three houses appeared to their right and a seared landscape of dirt and rocks stretched to the escarpment blocking the valley's end.

"There's no place to hide! We've got to run for it!" shouted Juan, setting off at a rapid pace. Dressed in shorts, T-shirts, and running shoes, the twins were perfectly clothed and sped up the valley with long strides as years of athletics paid off. They were almost to the end of the canyon when another boom sounded and there was a clear buzz in the air above them. Looking back, they saw a man kneeling by the houses aiming a rifle at them.

"Spread apart and zig-zag!" yelled Juan. "Look for the cave!"

Their pace slowed because they were moving erratically, but in a few seconds Sophia spotted it.

"To the right! There it is!" she called as another boom sounded and yards behind them a puff of dust sprang up. A dark hole at the bottom of the cliff marked the opening and they dashed to it, throwing themselves inside.

"Get away from the cave mouth," cautioned Juan pulling Sophia to the side. "It's a perfect target. Have you got your cell phone? I left mine in the van."

"Yes," she panted, wide eyed. The stress of being shot at had exacerbated the exertion of running.

"Turn on the flashlight We need to keep moving," he said, getting to his feet. Pulling the phone from her pocket, Sophia swiped the screen and a beam of light broke the darkness. She set out toward the back of the cave and suddenly stopped. The wall to their left was covered in paintings. There were likenesses of all sorts of animals drawn in large and small scale. Among them were clear portrayals of hunters armed with bows or spears. The paintings extended along the whole length of the wall and included the almost full-size human image that had scared Cuto nearly 400 years ago.

"It's just as Great Grandfather described," she murmured, awestruck. Despite the urgency of their situation, she couldn't help sweeping the light across the rock to reveal the incredible display. For a moment both of them were mesmerized until the faint sound of another shot reverberated down the cave.

CHAPTER 41

The Shaft

"We need to keep moving," said Juan, roused from his reverie. "Maybe there'll be time to study the paintings later." Directing the light toward the back of the cave, Sophia saw what seemed to be a blank wall but she advanced confidently. Sure enough, a slab of rock extended from the left wall, giving the impression that it was the end of the cave; however, behind it was a space, big enough to walk along, that angled to the left.

"There's no sound of water," muttered Juan as they made their way behind the slab. "The spring must have finally dried up like the others."

After a few yards they came to a dead end. Sophia flashed the light down to the right and left.

"See, there's where the water came through and exited toward the canyon!" she exclaimed in a hushed voice. "This is unbelievable!"

"Are you thinking what I am?" asked Juan. Like many twins, they often knew each other's thoughts.

"Yes, of course, the hand-holds." She held the light on the opposing face. It showed two sets of slots, carved in the rock about a foot apart, ascending into the dark toward a small circle of light far above. Each slot was cut at a slight downward angle, to create a secure hold for hand or foot, and was offset slightly from the opposing hole to promote rapid climbing.

"It's the escape shaft," said her brother. "We need to go up; that guy's coming after us. I'll hold the light for you."

Sophia put her hands into opposing holes and followed suit with her feet. She found the grooves, protected from the elements for centuries, easy to grip and secure. For the first few feet she was tentative, but soon fell into a rhythm of changing hand and footholds alternately, creating a steady ascent of the shaft. Even when she lost the benefit of light from the phone, she found the ancient holes to be so regularly spaced that she was able to move comfortably toward the small patch of sky far above.

"I'm right behind you," murmured Juan as they moved up the shaft in total darkness. Minutes went by and the daylight got larger until Sophia was at the top of the shaft. As she moved one hand over the lip, it encountered a hole cut into the horizontal rock surface, making it easy to climb right onto the desert floor. In a minute Juan was standing beside her. Around them was a pile of rocks and rubble about two feet high; beyond, the desert stretched away to a low range of hills in the west. Scattered about were a few saguaro cactuses and 30 yards behind them yawned the vast hole marking the hidden canyon. Juan moved quickly to the rim and lying on his stomach, peered down.

"He just went into the cave," he murmured. "If he has any kind of light, he'll find the shaft. We need to see if he's coming." Returning to the pile of rocks, both of them stretched out and peeped into the hole. Long minutes passed and only blackness met their gaze. Just as Juan had concluded that the man hadn't found the streambed, a tiny flicker of light showed far below!

"He must have a cigarette lighter or matches," whispered Sophia as they eased their heads back from the opening.

"He'll see the handholds and know how we escaped," replied Juan. "We've got to be ready. The medallion's heating up again."

Ten minutes later a head covered with long blond hair, cautiously emerged at the top of the shaft. Narrow-set eyes squinted in the sun above a hooked nose; scraggly beard and dirt covered a face grinning in triumph. Lifting himself from the hole, the man remained crouched behind the rocks as he removed the assault rifle from his back. Rising slowly, he stared about him at the desert. Nothing moved in the vast expanse, save a small bird flitting about a tall cactus nearby.

"You can't escape!" he yelled. "There's nowhere to go in the desert. Make it easy on yourselves so I don't have to hurt you." Silence answered him. "All right, if that's the way you want it. They've got me on a murder charge, so I've got nothing to lose. It's your life."

"Don't shoot, I give up," yelled Juan, getting to his feet from behind a large rock 60 feet to the right of the convict. He raised his hands in the air. "Don't shoot!"

"Where's the other one?"

"What other one?" asked Juan.

"Don't play with me, kid, or you're dead!" shouted the man, raising his rifle as a strange whirring sounded behind him. "What the…" he said, starting to turn.

"Run!" screamed Juan, sprinting away.

"I warned you kid," yelled the convict, swinging back and raising the rifle. The gun was halfway up when a tremendous blow struck him from behind, fracturing his right shoulder blade. Screaming in pain, the man dropped the rifle and fell to his knees as another missile hurtled into his left shoulder with the same result. He slumped forward passing out.

Sling whirling, Sophia advanced from the saguaro behind which she had been hiding, but there was no need for another throw. She remained alert, however, until her brother had retrieved the rifle, as well as a pistol stuck in the man's belt.

"You timed it perfectly," she said calmly. "He never got turned enough to see me before you distracted him by running. I had time for a full five revolutions with the sling."

"I'm amazed the impact didn't knock him flat," replied Juan. "That rock was going so fast I couldn't see it!"

"A little bigger rock would have laid him out," agreed his sister grimly.

CHAPTER 42

Spooked

Twenty minutes later the twins were crouched at the rim of the main canyon, staring down at the vehicles, having left their unconscious assailant securely tied hand and foot with strips of cloth ripped from the man's heavy flannel shirt. They could see the students sitting against the van with Mike on one end, Mr. Ramos and Thomas on the other. One of the convicts was leaning against a rock facing them. Even from a distance they could see water bottles and their lunch packages scattered around him. The other convict was making his way toward the pile of rubble below them. He climbed the rocks and, cupping his hands, shouted into the passageway. After waiting a few minutes, he called to his friend and pointed to the opening before clambering down the far side of the rubble and entering the crack.

"Let's follow him," said Juan, pushing back from the edge and standing up. As they made their way along the lip of split in the canyon wall, Sophia noticed a large pile of rock ahead.

"Look!" she exclaimed in excitement. "There's one of the piles Cuto made to dump into the passageway!" Indeed, as they drew close, several shards of wood, gray and weathered, poked from the pile.

"Those must be the remains of poles set to start the avalanche. I can't believe they haven't completely disintegrated," murmured Juan in awe.

"Maybe it's the dry climate," said his sister. "Probably there were long ends sticking out to lever the boulders off the edge, but there are just scraps now."

Occasionally peering down, the twins tracked the convict from above until he emerged into the side canyon. As he stepped into the sunlight, he shaded his eyes and shouted something into the dry, barren valley.

"He's too far away to see the cave," whispered Juan, as they lay side-by-side staring at the man 200 feet below. As they watched, he bent down and picked an object off the ground, examined it, and shouted again.

"I'll bet he found one of the shells from the other guy firing at us," Juan speculated. "But he doesn't know what to do because his friend's not answering."

However, the convict began walking slowly up the canyon floor, head bent.

"He's following the tracks," Sophia said softly. The man covered 50 yards and bent over to retrieve another object from the ground. "He's found another shell," she added. Now the convict began walking confidently up valley, stopping occasionally to scan the ground and stare at the base of the cliffs ahead, already shadowed from the lowering sun.

"He's going to find the cave," muttered Juan, "but maybe he won't be able to figure it out."

"He can follow our tracks," observed Sophia. "The question is whether he'll risk the shaft in the growing dark." The man was moving more cautiously as he entered the deep shadows, the twins keeping pace above, careful not to expose more than the tops of their heads. Suddenly the figure below stopped and stared intently ahead.

"He's seen the cave," whispered Juan. Raising his rifle, the convict walked slowly toward the opening and gave another shout. "He doesn't know if we've somehow managed to get the other rifle and are in there waiting for him," he continued, "there's been no word from his friend."

There was a flicker of light below as the man crouched and thrust an arm into the cave, pointing his rifle into the entrance with the other arm. He finally went to his knees and crawled inside. The twins were starting to get up and head for the top of the escape shaft when there was a muffled 'boom' from below; they scrambled back just in time to see the man scuttle out of the cave and throw himself to one side behind a rock, weapon leveled at the opening. After a confused minute, a low giggle escaped from Sophia.

"I'll bet he shot at the painting that scared Cuto!" she gasped, struggling to keep her voice down. There was silence for a moment before Juan replied.

"I think you're right! Look at him; he's ready to defend himself. If he was really worried about an attack, in the wavering light the painting could have scared him and he shot at it, probably dropping his lighter in the process!" he chuckled. As they watched in the deepening shadow, the convict showed no inclination to re-enter the cave; in fact, 20 minutes later he began a wide detour along the south wall of the canyon and headed for the passageway.

CHAPTER 43

Under Cover
of Darkness

FROM THE ROCK LOOKOUT station, the twins stared
through the dark at the fire built by the convicts from
wood Mike had brought to shore up his well. The two
men sat on rocks warming their hands in the blaze,
while the students and adults remained on the ground
alongside the van. Shadowing the second man from
above until he returned to the vehicles, the twins had
gone back and descended the shaft, ignoring dire
threats shouted at them by the now conscious but
securely bound escapee. Aided by brilliant stars, they'd
made their way down the valley and through the crack.
Using the utmost care to be quiet, the two had eased
over the rubble and into the sheltering boulders.

"What are we going to do?" Sophia had questioned during their walk down the valley.

"Remember the Apache attack on Cuto, Backward Looking, and Walks in the Grass? I think we should do the same thing in reverse. They were going toward the passageway, we'll split up and come from it," he said, and continued to outline his plan. "Those men will never expect us and we'll have the advantage of the dark."

"I like it," she'd responded. "And this time I'm using a bigger rock."

After watching the fire for a few moments, Juan touched his sister lightly on the shoulder and slipped between the boulders into the dark. He made his way past the pile of rubble and along the base of the wall in a down-valley direction. After waiting a minute, Sophia eased from the lookout and crept up valley along the escarpment. Both moved slowly, careful not to dislodge stones and treading quietly on soft dirt wherever possible. Protected by the inky darkness at the base of the cliffs, they were practically invisible.

After 50 yards, Sophia left the security of the cliff and moved slowly out into the canyon above the cars. She kept low to the ground, almost crawling, and moved only a few feet at a time. Unfortunately there were no cacti, bushes, or trees to hide her: only a few rocks and small patches of grass decorated the valley floor. In daylight she would have been completely visible; however, the circle of light from the fire put everything beyond it in darkness and she was confident the men wouldn't spot her. When she was directly up-valley from the fire, she crept toward it until she was yards away. To her left was the backhoe, its arm extended forward, bucket resting on the ground. Holding her watch close, Sophia saw by the luminous dial that 25 minutes had passed since she left the rocks.

"Good," she thought, "Juan allowed us 45 minutes to get in place." Stretching the loaded sling out on the ground next to her, she lay flat to avoid creating a silhouette. Minutes dragged by. When her watch showed it was time, Sophia eased herself to a crouch, right hand gripping the sling, left hand holding a second rock. Facing the backhoe, she swung the sling once and hurled a rock at it. Her aim was good and the rock rattled around the cockpit loudly.

"What was that?" yelled one of the convicts as both leaped up grabbing their rifles.

"Aaaggg!" screamed the other, crumpling to the ground as a nearly point-blank missile from Juan's sling shattered his knee. The first man whirled around, looking back at the cliff, only to have Sophia's second rock slam into his hip, splintering bone and tissue. He toppled with a cry of agony as Mike and Thomas raced forward to grab the rifles while both convicts writhed on the ground, lost in agony. There was a loud cheer from the kids as Juan and Sophia walked into the firelight, loaded slings dangling from their hands.

"How did you do that?" questioned the ranch hand incredulously.

"It's an old-fashioned weapon," replied Juan, holding up the sling. "It can be deadly if you know how to use it. We practice almost daily."

"It's one of the oldest weapons in the world," said Thomas, staring at the sling. "But I've never seen anyone wield it before. Until now," he added, "but then I really didn't see it in the dark!"

"Sophia will give you a demonstration sometime," promised Juan. "She's done most of the damage today."

"Oh?"

"Yeah, the third guy is up there on the desert with two broken shoulder blades," he said, as the men and students gawked at him. "We'll tell you all about it, but you need to know my sister's awesome!" he grinned as Sophia flushed bright red.

CHAPTER 44

Great Grandfather's Surprise

"So that's what took place, Great Grandfather," Juan concluded as the twins started to clear away breakfast dishes at the old man's house a week later. "We didn't want to risk killing those guys by hitting them in the head, so the knee and hip shots had to be accurate or they would have started shooting. We talked about it on the way home: even though there was only firelight to see by, our throws were dead-on because of the hundreds of hours we've practiced over the last 20 months."

"It happened really fast," Sophia added. "We'd planned which convict each of us would target, but once the rock hit the backhoe, there was no time to think. I had to reload and start swinging while Juan was knocking down the first man. It was all about relying on muscle memory to execute the throw."

"I would never have chosen that experience for you," said their relative, "but now you know what it was like for your ancestors to be in battle. I'm proud of you. You responded just as every one of them did."

"It was so incredible to walk the very ground they did!" exclaimed Sophia. "I'm not sure we could have climbed to the cliff dwelling the way we climbed the secret shaft because the handholds were badly worn, but everything was there exactly as you described. We could see the marks in the cliff coming down from the desert and there was discoloration way over on the right, which we guessed came from the spring that supplied the Anasazi with water."

"The archeologist, Thomas, thought the ruins down valley were from Anasazi farmers living there because of the distance to the cliff house," said Juan. "But we knew it was the remains of the Aztec village that grew up in support of Cuto and Ria. We were already on our way to look for the passage when the convicts showed up."

"We've talked about what both canyons would have been like with water," Sophia exclaimed. "With grass, cottonwoods, and wildlife, it must have been gorgeous! We understand why the family stayed so long."

"Not only that, but the cave and escape shaft were amazing," declared her brother. "The paintings have to be an archeological treasure! And the footholds in the shaft are as good as when they were carved! It was like walking right into the stories…except for the guy shooting at us," he added ruefully.

"I just can't imagine why Mr. Rodriguez allowed us to go in," Sophia stated. "Nobody but Thomas and a few trusted students have seen the place and they had only explored the cliff house." There was a long pause.

"I asked him to," said the old man. There was an even longer pause as the twins stared at Great Grandfather with open mouths.

"You asked him to let us in?" Juan finally stammered.

"Yes. I called him after Sophia called me about your experience at the Plaza. I thought the medallion might have had something to do with it and decided you should experience the setting our family lived in for generations. If the two of you are the Chosen Ones, as I suspect, perhaps associating with the past would trigger a key to unlocking the medallion's secret."

"But…how do you even know Mr. Rodriguez?" the youth fumbled for words. "We thought you'd lived your whole life in the San Luis Valley."

"Well, not exactly my whole life," smiled the old man, "but a good deal of my life has been here. Mr. Rodriguez' grandfather was one of my closest friends when I was a child." He settled back in his chair and took a sip of coffee. "But that's another story."

CHAPTER 45

The Coast

Tukor never tired of watching waves break against the shore. He stood for hours at the water's edge, or high on a promontory overlooking the ocean, watching line after line of great rollers crash against the huge rocks and cliffs scattered along the shoreline. Tikaani explained tides and at low tide he would walk on the damp sand watching Shadow dash about and chase crabs. Overhead, hundreds of gulls wheeled and dived, hoping for a morsel from the shells the black wolf cracked apart. Returning to camp, he would sit and stare at the sweeping expanse of gray extending to the western horizon and wonder where it ended. He was stunned by the size of the ocean; the stories hadn't prepared him for such a vast panorama.

Tikaani went north to locate a village; he was in his element now and anxious to find people to assist him with preparations for traveling home. Until he returned, Tukor's only concern was to provide food for himself and the wolf. Hunting was easy in the forest teeming with elk, allowing most days to be spent studying the coastline. From the promontory, he could see dozens of large brown animals lying on great rocks just beyond the breaking surf. Frequently they would squirm off their perches and cavort about in the surging water. The Inuit called them seals and had explained that they were an important source of food and materials for people living near the ocean. Twice he saw enormous gray and white fish burst from the ocean to snatch a seal right off the edge of its rock.

But it was the occasional plumes of white puffing from the sea that fascinated him most. They arose from huge dark bodies that briefly broke the surface of the water before disappearing again beneath it. He learned the plumes would often reappear, moments later, at some distance from where he first spotted them.

"Is that the animal the traders described to Lita?" he wondered. "How would you hunt such a creature?" When he saw a gigantic tail lift to slap the water with a tremendous shower of spray, he just shook his head. "I must ask Tikaani about these fish," he thought.

"They're called 'whales,'" said the Inuit when he returned days later. "One of them will feed a village for weeks."

"How do you hunt them?" asked Tukor in awe.

"We use boats like the one we rode on the river, but much larger," replied Tikaani. "They carry eight men to paddle, another to steer, and a hunter up front. The boat maneuvers close to the whale and the hunter hurls a long spear into it. It's very dangerous because the canoes are unstable and the animals are so strong: one blow of its tail or flukes will destroy the boat."

"Flukes?"

"Flukes are huge fins, like the ones you see on trout. When a whale rolls on its side a fluke can come out of the water and strike the boat."

"Have you hunted whales?" inquired Tukor.

"The year after I was captured would have been the first year I was allowed to hunt them," Tikaani answered wistfully…

He had returned from a village a week's travel up the coast where he had been well received. The next day the two men hid their canoe in the forest, assembled their gear in large packs and set out. They made good time through the countryside and arrived some days later at a community located a short distance from the sea. Tukor stared in amazement as they approached. Instead of teepees, here were long wooden houses with gently sloping roofs upon which rocks had been scattered.

"These are the Makah people," explained Tikaani. "They get much of their food from the sea and are expert whale hunters." The New Mexican's eyes gleamed; whale hunters were the very people he wanted to meet.

As they entered the village, a pack of dogs surrounded Shadow. These were not the usual scrawny animals of the Plains Indian communities. They were bigger and stronger, colored in whites and grays. While the others formed a circle around the wolf, the dominant male advanced with bared teeth, growling deep in his throat. Shadow stood his ground, hackles raised, a warning snarl ripping from his chest. The dog stopped about three feet away, crouching slightly, ears laid back. He was almost as tall as the wolf and thicker through the shoulders and chest. Shadow watched, eyes blazing.

Suddenly the dog drove in, seeking the wolf's throat, only to snap at the air as the big animal leaped aside with incredible speed and laid open the leader's left shoulder with slashing teeth. The dog yelped and whirled to meet the attack, but he was too late; there was a brief but violent entangling of black and gray, accompanied by hideous snarling, and a minute later the dog lay on the ground, his throat ripped open. Shadow, blood dripping from his muzzle, turned to face the next challenge but the pack was already groveling in submission to its new leader.

CHAPTER 46

Learning to Swim

INSIDE THE GREAT WOODEN houses were a number of hearths and Tukor realized each structure housed several families. Shown to a vacant living space, they put their packs down and followed their guide toward a small bay visible through the trees. The enclosed harbor was about 300 yards wide and completely surrounded by land, except for a narrow opening to the rolling sea beyond. A couple of long wooden dugouts were drawn up on the gravelly beach. Each was made from the hollowed-out trunk of a single tree. The wood had been shaped with a sculpted, jutting bow, and the sides of each displayed carved images.

"It's a perfect spot for the boats," Tikaani pointed out. "Even in a violent storm, the water here stays calm." Shadow trotted off to smell the area around the dugouts. "It looks like your friend picked up the scent of seals brought in by those boats," he observed.

Before long, a dugout appeared in the channel, paddles rising and falling in perfect unison to the rhythm of a song the men were singing. As they reached the beach, the men jumped out and hauled out the bodies of two seals before dragging the boat clear of the water.

"I saw those animals on rocks near the river mouth," said the New Mexican, strolling over to take a close look at the seals.

"In the north, we hunt them in small one-man boats. They have to be dragged in to shore by the hunter, without the benefit of strong men like these to carry them in a dugout," explained Tikaani.

Word was sent to the village and soon people gathered to skin and butcher the seals. The village dogs also arrived, but kept their distance until the black wolf had filled himself with bits of meat discarded by the sharp knives. As with buffalo, almost every part of the animals would be used by the Makah.

Shortly, another boat appeared in the channel and approached the beach. There were no seals on board, but a number of large fish were tossed to the ground. A short, powerfully built man jumped from the bow and approached the visitors. There were streaks of gray in his long black hair and his eyes were keen and discerning. He grasped Tikaani's forearm in greeting and turned toward Tukor.

"I am Hatch," he said, pausing for the Inuit to interpret, "leader of this village. Your friend is from the far north but we share many of the same practices, living by the sea. He has described how you rescued him from those in the south to whom he was sold. We welcome you."

"Tikaani and I have a special connection," replied Tukor.

"I see," acknowledged the Makah chief, glancing at Shadow. "He told me he knew you had come for him."

"I'd like to go out with the hunters," said the New Mexican. "Chasing whales seems like running down buffalo."

"I've never hunted buffalo," said Hatch, "but whales are extremely dangerous. We're planning a hunt soon and I'll discuss your involvement tonight." With that, they all lent a hand carrying the day's catch to the village.

When they joined Hatch at his hearth in the longhouse that evening, he'd discarded the heavy clothing worn at sea. Against his bare chest hung a small whale carved from ivory and a great white scar crossed the top of his bare left forearm.

"So you wish to go with the hunters after whales," he said, gesturing for them to sit across the fire from him.

"Yes, my family has wanted to see the ocean for generations, since first hearing about it from traders," replied the New Mexican. "They spoke of great fish, as long as many horses standing front to back, and we obtained carvings of them like the one hanging from your neck."

"Did the traders describe the danger in hunting these creatures?" asked the other.

"Not in the tales I've heard," admitted Tukor. "They entice with stories about mysterious places, but don't reveal the hardships."

"That's because they want to interest you in their goods," said Hatch. "We like the warm robes they bring, but never hear about the difficulty of hunting buffalo."

"Lives are sometimes lost in buffalo hunts," acknowledged the guest. "But we don't dwell on the dangers when exchanging robes for their goods."

"Even so," said Hatch, "we don't discuss the risks of going after whales. We're more interested in the barter. Do you swim?" The question caught Tukor by surprise.

"Uhh, no," he answered haltingly. He knew how to splash about in a river to get clean, but had never actually learned to propel himself through the water. He glanced at the impassive Inuit beside him and thought he detected mirth in the dark eyes. "Why do you ask?"

"One cannot go in the boats unless he can swim," answered Hatch gravely. "Should the boat overturn, one has to swim to stay alive."

"Then I will learn to swim," Tukor announced decisively.

"Good," smiled the chief. After a minute, he added with a twinkle in his eye, "You will have excellent teachers."

The next morning when they emerged from the longhouse a group of children surrounded Tukor, jabbering and pointing toward the ocean. He looked questioningly at Tikaani.

"These are your instructors," explained the Inuit, trying to keep his face serious.

"But, they're only children!" cried the New Mexican.

"They're like little seals in the water," exclaimed Tikaani. "You'd better go with them; Hatch has probably offered them some reward for turning you into a good swimmer!" Even as he spoke some of the bolder children were pulling on Tukor's clothing and gesturing for him to follow them. Resigned to his fate, he followed them toward the bay. About halfway there a small hand was thrust into each of his and he looked down to see two little girls, no more than six years old, smiling up at him.

When they reached the beach, the kids all threw their clothes on the ground and dashed into the water. The day was chill and overcast but they seemed not to mind, splashing and swimming about like a school of fish. Tukor, determined not to be out-done by a bunch of children, flung off his clothes and waded stark naked, save headband and medallion, into the water. It was cold and he was gasping by the time he got waist deep. The two little girls paddled over and motioned for him to put his head under water. As he lowered himself inch by inch, he found his legs suddenly yanked from beneath him and he plunged below the surface; two of the older kids had dived from behind and dislodged his feet! Yelling and spluttering, he managed to get righted and stand up…all the children were laughing.

After a few minutes, the two girls swam by him demonstrating a dog paddle and Tukor gingerly lowered himself into the water and tried to copy them. At the end of an hour he was able to make his way along the bay with increasing confidence, staying in shallow water and accompanied by the whole crowd of children shouting encouragement. His movements were jerky and he kept his head out of the water, but determination kept him going until the kids decided the lesson was over. As he walked back to the longhouses, surrounded by his new friends, the man from the south felt a great sense of accomplishment.

Thereafter the pattern was established: every morning Tukor and his gaggle of instructors would head for the bay for hours of swimming lessons. In the beginning he was absolutely exhausted from the exercise and cold but gradually he adapted, as the kids had, and began to look forward to the sessions. Games of tag helped him transition to an overhand stroke by making him extend his arms and reach in order to catch even the slowest of the children. Within two weeks they moved him into deeper water, where he learned to dive and make his way under water with great sweeps of his arms and frog-like motions of his legs. Tikaani often watched from shore, amazed at the progress of his companion. After a month, the children reported to Hatch that the New Mexican was ready for the big dugouts.

CHAPTER 47
Seal Hunt

"The traders are late this year," remarked Hatch conversationally as he regarded the three men across the hearth. They had gathered for the purpose of assigning Tukor to a boat for a seal hunt the following day. The most skilled harpooner in the village, a man named Talon, had been summoned for the occasion.

"Perhaps they were attacked by thieves," suggested Tukor, remembering years when traders had showed up at the pueblo empty handed.

"Perhaps," replied the chief, "but they don't bring food, so we still need to hunt.

I would like our guest to ride with you tomorrow," he continued, addressing Talon. "The children say he is a capable swimmer, although the faster ones can still elude him, and able to survive in the event the boat capsizes." The harpooner, stocky and obviously possessing great strength, nodded.

"I'll have him sit directly in front of the sweep," he said. "He'll be able to observe everything from there." Tikaani had already explained to his friend that even though he was now able to swim, the Makah would allow him to be a passenger, but not a participant yet in the hunt.

"The dugouts are quite unstable," he'd described. "Paddling requires precise coordination and discipline between eight men; any action on one side, if not countered on the other, can cause the boat to roll over. The men are directed by a ninth in the stern, who wields a long sweep paddle and is responsible for maneuvering the craft. His commands are instantly called out during the action of a hunt; however, when the boat is simply traveling he has the crew sing to establish a cadence. Tikaani explained that the paddlers were not positioned across from each other but in an irregular pattern, according to weight and strength, to further increase stability. Adding to the problem was the violent motion of the harpooner as he hurled his weapon from the bow. "To you it will all seem measured and easy," declared the Inuit, "but it takes months of practice to develop a smooth team."

As he walked with Talon and his crew toward the dugout the next morning, Tukor was filled with excitement, touched with a bit of dread. His swimming lessons had never exceed a depth of 10 feet, and now he was about to embark on the surface of what was to him a bottomless ocean. The harpooner's warning to remain still in the boat was unnecessary; Tikaani's words about the instability of the dugouts had already created resolve that he wouldn't move a muscle once he'd taken his position.

They all pushed the boat out into the water, where four paddlers on each side steadied it while Talon, the sweep, and Tukor climbed aboard. Talon went forward and the sweep directed the New Mexican to sit directly in front of him in the back of the boat. The craft was narrower in bow and stern, so Tukor was able to place one hand on either gunwale for balance. By twos, the opposing paddlers swung aboard so effortlessly there was no lurch to either side and, in less than a minute, the dugout was underway.

"Their precision is like that of skilled horsemen," Tukor thought to himself. "One never sees the hours of work that go towards developing skills." As they passed through the channel and onto the open sea, his fears dissipated in the thrill of easily riding ocean swells under the powerful strokes of the paddlers. The day was clear, a few white clouds set against the blue sky, with the inevitable flocks of gulls wheeling and diving overhead. A sense of exhilaration swept over him as he realized he was living the dreams of his great, great grandmother Lita.

When they returned to the little bay that afternoon, three dead seals carefully arranged between the paddlers, Tukor felt a sense of regret the adventure was over. The hunt had taken them miles along the coast to a spot where a cluster of great flat rocks rose from the sea just offshore. As they approached, numerous seals had launched themselves into the water from their perches in the warm sun. The water was rough around the rocks, as the swells broke on them before rushing to the shore, and Talon had gestured to proceed slowly. Under the commands of the sweep, the men had skillfully kept the dugout balanced in the roiling water while moving it gently forward. The harpooner stood in the bow, lance raised in his right hand, left hand giving signals to the men behind where he wanted to go. The seals scattered in the water as the boat drew near and Tukor watched in fascination as Talon directed them dangerously close to an enormous rock. Suddenly the harpooner's arm flashed forward, driving the shaft into the water in front of him; simultaneously, the paddlers eased the boat backward away from the threatening rock. Line attached to the harpoon sped over the bow from a large coil at Talon's feet; when it began to slow he grabbed it and leaned back to stop the stricken seal's dive.

"Most of them will dive out of reach," the sweep had explained, "but there's usually one that becomes curious and swims up, particularly near the safety of the rocks. Once harpooned, it will die from drowning rather than return to the surface." Sure enough, after some time the line went slack and Talon began pulling the dead animal in.

When the prey was safely laid in the bottom of the boat the hunt began again, but success was difficult. The rough water, combined with the quickness of the seals, often conspired to make the harpooner miss, and it took several hours to kill two more animals. Nevertheless, the expedition had been a success and the men sang in rhythm with the paddles all the way home. As they dragged the seals to the village, Tukor asked the harpooner if he could ride along on the next whale hunt.

"I'll talk to Hatch," was all Talon would say.

CHAPTER 48

Qimmiq

A week later, the routine of the village was disturbed by the excited cries of the children announcing the arrival of the traders. When Tukor and Tikaani joined the crowd at the edge of the village, the first thing they noticed was a large pile of buffalo robes, colorful blankets, and gourds of every size and shape. Several horses grazed close by and a small man was arranging a large deerskin on the ground in front of the goods.

"It looks like there's only one trader," commented Tukor, staring at the scene. "It reminds me of the pueblo near home." He glanced at the horses and stopped in his tracks, staring fixedly at the animals. "That's the gray mare that belonged to Elk's Tooth: the one we

thought would make a great buffalo runner! It must
be the same trader who brought the request for horses
from Crooked Horn!" He turned toward his friend,
but the Inuit was already staring intently at the trader.

Suddenly, Tikaani was striding rapidly forward
through the crowd. Reaching the trader, he touched
him on the shoulder and bent down to peer at the face
raised toward him in a twisted manner to compensate
for loss of a left eye. The old man slowly straightened,
staring with his good eye at the figure before him. The
people became silent as the two exchanged words in
a strange language. When they embraced, a murmur
ran through the watching Makah. It was clear that
something very important had just transpired. Tikaani
turned toward them, eyes glistening.

"This is my father, Qimmiq. He was wounded and
left for dead in the attack on our people when I was
young. I was made a slave and taken far to the south,
where there is great heat and little water. When he
recovered, he became a trader and searched for me for
many years. He finally learned where I was, but the
Comanche hid me when he came and wouldn't give
me up. Only when Tukor arrived with his black wolf
was I able to escape…and now we are together again."
A great shout went up from the people as tears ran
down the weathered face of the old trader.

"Tonight we will have a feast to celebrate this
reunion," announced Hatch with a smile. "Our friend

has been bringing his buffalo robes for many years to warm our bodies and now he has warmed our hearts!" And indeed, the feasting, songs, and dancing went on late into the night around a huge bonfire in the center of the village.

In the days that followed, the tribe learned that Qimmiq had been delayed for several weeks at a village to the south, near the mouth of the great river. His buffalo robes had traded at a premium because the people were short of clothing for the coming winter. In return he had collected many colorful beads unlike any he had seen before, four knives with extremely sharp metal blades, and two small rectangular pieces of glass, which he kept carefully stored in a buckskin pouch. When he displayed the beads and knives, the Makah people hurriedly scattered to find their best shells and carvings to offer in trade. The pieces of glass were only revealed privately one evening at the chief's hearth.

"What's this?" asked Hatch as Qimmiq carefully handed him the small rectangle.

"Look at it," said the trader. There was a sharp intake of breath as the leader complied. He touched the silvered glass with a forefinger.

"It's like looking at your image in a pool of still water...except it's solid," exclaimed Hatch in amazement, handing it over for the others to see.

"Do they have more of these in the village?' asked Tukor, thinking of his Crow and Cheyenne friends.

"Possibly," replied the trader. "But I think they will need more than a buffalo robe."

"Then they shall have it," declared the New Mexican, thinking of two beautiful serapes he still had in the packs.

The next day Tukor borrowed the gray mare and a packhorse from Qimmiq and headed south. There was talk of a whale hunt during the coming moon and he wanted to travel as fast as possible. Hatch had given him two seal skins and an ivory bear to trade for another of the pieces of glass, or any other item he thought the chief could use. Tikaani stayed behind to help his father with the trading and settle him at their hearth for the coming winter.

It felt good to be riding again and the gray was energetic and attentive to the expertise she sensed from him. Freed from the constraints of the village, Shadow bounded happily through the forest for a time before settling down to a steady pace beside the horse. In two days they covered what had taken six days on foot weeks before.

Qimmiq's directions led him to a spot further up the river from where he and Tikaani had camped when they reached the ocean. He vaguely remembered passing a small village during their last day in the canoe but realized that his focus had been on the vast stretch of water ahead. Thus, he was surprised to see a much larger camp than he expected, and even more surprised by the men walking forward to meet him.

Although dressed in buckskins like Indians, they were taller, bearded, and white skinned. One of them casually held what Tukor recognized as a musket in the crook of his arm, but the others bore no weapons. All were smiling in a friendly way, although they stopped several yards away in deference to the wolf. One of them stepped forward and raised a hand in greeting, speaking words in a strange language. The New Mexican raised his hand in return.

"Greetings! I've come to trade," announced Tukor, using the language of the Makah. The man shook his head, so Tukor repeated the message in Crow, then Ute; each attempt was met by shake of the head from the man, until one of his companions said some words that sounded vaguely familiar. Switching to Spanish, Tukor restated his overture, causing yet another of the men to smile widely and respond.

"We thought you might speak French, but instead it's Spanish!" he said. "That's a tongue we haven't encountered on our journey. You are welcome in our camp!" There was a brief pause as he interpreted the conversation to the rest of the group.

"I live far away in the south where the Spanish have many villages," explained Tukor. "They've not always been friendly, but we speak their language." The man nodded knowingly.

"Your horses look similar to those of a trader who recently visited us."

"They're the same animals. He acquired them from the Pueblo Indians in the desert, but he lent them to me as the stock originally came from the herd of my father and mother," explained the New Mexican, sliding from the gray.

"You raise fine horses," replied the other appreciatively. He gestured at the man who had originally tried to start the conversation. "I would like to introduce one of our two leaders, Captain Clark."

CHAPTER 49

The Button

GREAT GRANDFATHER PAUSED slightly and was met by an outburst from Juan.

"No way!" he cried, almost shouting. "You've got to be kidding!"

"I'm not," said the old man. "But you ought to be a bit more courteous about interrupting a good story," he added with a grin, reaching for his coffee. Sophia sat stock still, eyes wide at the bombshell.

"Senor Clark," she finally stammered. "As in Lewis and Clark?"

"The very same," chuckled the old man.

"You mean to tell me that our family met what is probably the most famous expedition in the history of the country?" Juan's voice still rang with high volume.

"Not only that, but did some business with it," answered the storyteller quietly. "In fact, we think he showed them a thing or two and even won a bet!" The two stared at him as though he'd lost his mind.

"No one will believe this," muttered Juan, shaking his head. "If it weren't for you, I wouldn't believe it!"

"No one has to believe it," answered Great Grandfather. "It's part of the cherished history of our family, important to us alone."

"But Great Grandfather, this is so incredible! We're part of the history of the United States," whispered Sophia. She leaned forward, tears in her eyes.

"You'll never find us in the history books," said the old man wryly, "because The Corps of Discovery Expedition had many important things to discover and report. The brief visit of one man wasn't significant except to us, his family."

"What happened?" pressed Juan. "You can't send us away until next Saturday. Not now! I'll fill your coffee cup." He jumped up and grabbed the pot from the stove.

Great Grandfather took a sip.

"You're right," he answered. "I should have waited, but I got so wrapped up in telling the scene I couldn't stop!" He resumed the narrative...

The men had many questions about how Tukor had come to be in the area and he had questions for them about where they had come from, so talk went on far into the night. The whites were singularly impressed with Shadow, who never left his owner's side and, despite his obvious heritage, remained calm in the presence of so many of them. A couple tentatively patted his head and, save the slightest move away from their hands, he quietly tolerated it.

The next morning when Tukor displayed the serapes, a number of the men brought forward articles to trade, among them quantities of beads, two pairs of scissors, several small knives and three large knives (all with steel blades), and two of the glass mirrors. He traded Hatch's seal skin and ivory bear carving for one of the mirrors, but try as he might, he couldn't talk Meriwether Lewis out of the last mirror—even offering one of the serapes for it. The leader explained that he might need it on the long trip home. In the end, the New Mexican accepted a large sack of beads, a pair of scissors, one small knife, and one large knife for each serape.

"You'd think I had talked them out of their last pair of moccasins," he joked with the interpreter as the lengthy negotiations came to a close. He was disappointed about not getting the glass mirror, but opportunity arose later that afternoon. Lewis was demonstrating the operation of a rifle when a Canadian goose flew low over the camp. Raising the weapon, Lewis fired, but the bird disappeared across the treetops to the snorts and laughter of the other men.

"I thought you said the musket never fails to bring down game," said Tukor. When this was translated, the other man shrugged.

"I was distracted by explaining how it works," he replied. "I rarely miss."

"The target was indeed small," said the visitor. When this was conveyed, there were snickers from the watchers because the goose was large and close. Lewis' face reddened slightly.

"I can hit a target in the air one third the size," he blustered.

"We kill birds in the air with our weapons, but make no great noise to scare the flock," Tukor said innocently. The watching men went quiet at the inference the rifle was inferior.

"What do you use?"

"This," said his visitor, unwrapping the sling from his waist. Lewis and the others stared in amazement.

"You can hit a flying bird with that?" said the Captain.

"Yes, desert birds are small and fast and one's stomach doesn't like to see them get away," Tukor grinned.

"I find it hard to believe," replied Lewis.

"Perhaps a wager?" suggested Tukor with a straight face. "My packhorse against your mirror?"

Meriwether Lewis hesitated. He knew that many Indians were skilled with the bow, but had never encountered a sling. The stranger who hunted with it must be accurate or his people wouldn't survive in the desert. A packhorse was tempting for their return trip, yet... After a long moment he came to a decision and, reaching into a pouch at his side, produced a large brass button from a uniform long since discarded.

"A wager, if you dare," said he. "Hit this in the air and the mirror is yours; miss and the horse is mine." The astonished men saw Tukor give a slight nod and place a rock in the sling. He walked about 15 yards away, swinging the weapon slowly over his head. Turning, he increased the revolutions until the straps whirred loudly.

"Whenever you're ready," he called in Spanish.

Upon receiving the word, Lewis threw the button into the air with all his strength. Up and up it rose, every eye fixed on it. At the very apex of the flight, when it was suspended for a fraction of a second, there was a loud "ping" and it flew off to land in the grass many yards away. A great hurrah went up from the assembled men and they rushed to Tukor, clapping him on the shoulders in approval. First among them was Meriwether Lewis, a huge smile on his face.

"I never would have believed it," he admitted, handing over the mirror. "We could use a man like you on the Expedition when we start home in the spring."

"The land and the people you've described fascinate me, but in the spring I will accompany a friend on a long journey of our own," replied Tukor. "Now, I have to join a whale hunt." The next morning he was gone.

"Did that really happen?" asked Juan. "Wouldn't there be some word of it in the journals?"

"Surely they noted every encounter with indigenous people," added Sophia.

"We'll never know about everything that was not entered in the journals," replied the old man, setting the cup down and rising to his feet. He left the kitchen for a few minutes. "But perhaps this will convince you," he said upon returning. He handed them a badly dented ancient brass button.

CHAPTER 50
Whales

When Tukor returned to the village, the people were in a high state of excitement. For several days a group of whales had been spotted moving back and forth in the ocean about a mile offshore. Tikaani explained that they were probably feeding and the Makah had accelerated preparations for a hunt.

"You returned just in time," he said. "Hatch has decided you can ride in the second boat."

"When do we leave?" Tukor was barely able to contain his excitement.

"Tomorrow at dawn."

That night, as the two of them made their way through the longhouse, they found people busily at work making great coils of strong hemp rope; blowing air into seal skins sewn tightly shut, until they resembled oblong fur balloons; sharpening harpoon heads and long lances. Tikaani explained that the inflated seal skins would be attached to the rope to slow the whale as it fled after being harpooned. Unlike the enthusiasm of the villagers in the afternoon, the atmosphere in the large dwelling was quiet and somber. Tukor realized it reflected both reverence for and fear of the great beasts the men would encounter the next day. Hatch greeted them quietly as he honed the long bone blade of a lance.

"I'll take the lead boat. You may ride as before with Talon. Tikaani has told us of the power in your silver piece; perhaps it will bring us luck," he glanced at the medallion exposed on the New Mexican's chest. In the warmth of the building, the men customarily shed their shirts and Tukor was no exception. He instinctively fingered the cool metal.

"May it be so," he murmured.

The next morning a raw wind was blowing from the north under leaden skies. Winter had started and the air was chill; all the men dressed in sealskin coats and pants, made with the fur on the inside. This clothing was both warm and effective against the bitter wind; later in the season they would add mittens and caps of the same material. The entire village gathered quietly on the beach to see them off. Everyone, including the children, knew the danger these men were facing. Tukor, a favorite with the kids since his swimming lessons, received many waves on his way to the dugout. Shadow, unhappy at the separation, lay beside Tikaani, head on legs, eyes following every move of his owner. After blessing both boats and crews, Hatch boarded his dugout and led the way across the bay toward the open sea.

Once outside the protection of the hills surrounding the bay, the paddlers worked hard to drive the boats against a quartering wind from starboard. Bits of foam blown from the crests of waves splattered everyone and the harpooners, braced in the bows, held hands cupped against their cheeks to block spray from their eyes. On and on they went, Talon trailing Hatch's boat by 50 yards, until the shore was only a thin line behind them. Now the lead craft slowed, until it was just maintaining position against the wind, and the trailing dugout followed suit. Every eye searched the ocean. Hours passed, the boats rising and falling on ragged four-foot swells, with the harpooners standing upright to scan the horizon... but nothing disturbed the great gray expanse. Pemmican was passed among the men and Tukor felt warmth expanding through his body, chilled despite the sealskin clothing.

All at once, Hatch pointed with his left arm and the crews saw several puffs of white briefly appear a quarter of a mile ahead. Hatch's men bent to their paddles and the boat surged forward. Talon motioned for his paddlers to follow and they closed the gap between

the two craft to 25 yards before settling to a rhythm
that matched the other's pace. Everyone focused on
Hatch, balanced at the very front of his boat, knees
slightly bent, the long shaft of the harpoon in his right
hand. He directed his men to angle left to intercept the
oncoming whales. Minutes dragged by.

Suddenly, Hatch gestured with his left hand for
more speed as a dark form became visible in the water
just ahead. His arm flashed forward as he hurled the
harpoon and the men quickly reversed their strokes to
pull clear of the whale. As the boat lurched backward,
Hatch abruptly bent over and began to pull in the rope
attached to the harpoon. The blade had skidded along
the whale's side and failed to penetrate. He waved for
Talon to go after the animals.

The paddlers needed no encouragement and the
second dugout sped forward. Braced in the rear, the
New Mexican saw Talon look to his right. Hatch had
attacked the lead whale, but others would be following.
Sure enough, the harpooner pointed and gestured for
the men to bring the boat slightly back into the wind.
So coordinated were the paddlers that the move was
made without direction from the sweep. Talon swept
his hand forward for more speed and the men bent to
their work. Suddenly, Tukor saw it: a great black form
passing in front of them about three feet below the
surface. Talon drove the harpoon down with all his
strength and the men began back-paddling as hard as

they could, but the last surge of speed made the craft sluggish to respond, too sluggish...

Out of the sea rose an enormous tail to tower above them. Talon frantically waved for the men to swing the bow left. The paddlers on that side stroked backward with all their might, water boiling around their blades, and the paddlers to the right dug blades forward with matching intensity. The sweep swung his long oar with desperate strokes and for an instant it looked like they were clear. Tukor, oblivious to the shouting and frenzied activity, could only watch in fascinated horror as the great tail began its descent. He had not truly understood how big the animals were and part of his mind was still struggling to deal with it as the enormous appendage seemed to plunge down in slow motion. As the black skin drew close, he clearly saw barnacles attached to it; then his world erupted in a chaotic tumult of noise, wind, and water.

Despite the last-ditch efforts of the men, the enormous tail brushed the gunwale to Talon's right before it slammed onto the water with a deafening crash. The wood split and the bow was driven down by the impact as though struck by a pile driver. The stern flipped up and forward, catapulting and scattering men in the air like so many dolls. The dugout appeared to stand on its head for an instant, then slid straight into the gray water, leaving no trace on the windblown ocean. The whole incident took less than 15 seconds.

CHAPTER 51
Doomed

WHEN THE STERN PITCHED forward, Tukor was launched like a cannonball, landing yards away with such force that he plunged completely under water. The seal skins briefly insulated him from the icy ocean, but quickly became waterlogged and began to drag him down. He kicked and stroked upward, but realized he was making no progress; he was sinking further and further into a murky darkness. In spite of the panic threatening to overwhelm him, he forced himself to stop struggling and focus on pulling the now burdensome jacket over his head. Yanking the garment this way and that, he finally worked his torso free and then pulled his arms from sleeves that seemed determined to cling. As the coat finally drifted away, a great beam of brilliant light suddenly illuminated the water. In it he could clearly see several men nearby struggling to free themselves from sealskins that threatened to drown them. Heads pivoted toward him and glancing down he realized the beam was coming from the medallion!

Yanking his leggings off, Tukor grabbed the medallion and flashed it at all the men he could see. He made a gesture for them to follow him and started for the surface. Free of the sealskins, his limbs easily propelled him upward, although by now he desperately needed air. As he rose, a body suddenly drifted into the great arc of light, blood streaming from its head. He swam toward it and recognized Talon; the light was so bright they could have been facing one another in the morning sun. The harpooner was unconscious, perhaps dead, with a large gash across the side of his head. Grabbing one of Talon's arms, the New Mexican kicked powerfully, stroking with his free hand. Just when he felt his lungs would burst, his head broke the surface. Gasping for air, he pulled Talon's head clear of the water and glanced about. He was in a trough between swells and when he rose to the top of the next wave there was no sign of the other boat.

Nearby other heads were visible in the ocean and he yelled hoarsely, kicking desperately and directing the medallion at them with his free hand. The Makah began swimming toward him, one of them dragging another wounded man. Within a short time they were all clustered in a loose circle. There were a total of eight, including him and Talon.

"Where are the others?" he croaked, barely able to speak. The men shook their heads. As he looked from one face to another, Tukor saw that their lips were already turning bluish: the bitterly cold water was taking its toll. Oddly, the men appeared calm. They knew the dangers of whale hunting and accepted the consequences of an accident. At the same time, he realized that the medallion was giving off a great heat. The water around his body was decidedly warm.

"Come closer!" he cried. "The silver is heating the water!" The men closed in until they formed a tight circle, arms across each other's shoulders. Tukor directed the beam around the inside of the circle. "Do you feel it?" he yelled against the wind. They each nodded in awe as the beam swept about their torsos and radiated heat. One of them suddenly shouted at the top of his lungs and pointed down with one hand.

"Below! Something brushed my feet!" Tukor ducked his head under water and aimed the medallion down. As the brilliant light illuminated the depths, he saw several very large fish swim away into the darkness.

"Sharks!" said one of the men grimly as the New Mexican raised his head, "Look." He pointed behind Tukor. Spinning around, the man from the desert saw a great fin slicing through the water toward him, from

40 feet away. As it drew to within 15 feet, an enormous light gray and white body rolled on its side displaying a fearsome mouth of teeth aimed right at him. There was no time to do anything but fling his hands in front of his face. In doing so, he lifted the medallion out of the water.

Most of the men later said they didn't see what happened because their eyes were temporarily blinded by a burst of light. All of them knew that regardless of who survived the first attack, the rest would quickly be torn apart by other white killers swarming to the blood. Only two men saw what happened. They described it to the villagers for so many years that it became a permanent part of the Makah legends.

"As the great white closed," they recounted in hushed tones, "Our visitor threw his arms in front of his face as if to ward off the attack. His amulet, which had been warming the water around us, dangled from one hand. All of a sudden, a brilliant bolt of fire, thick as a man's torso, erupted from the silver straight into the shark's open mouth! The 20 foot shark was propelled back through the water for yards before bursting completely apart in a tremendous blast of fire, flesh and blood. Almost immediately other sharks came rushing at the dead one and the water was stirred to foam in the feeding frenzy. In the chaos, a few of them must have bitten others, creating more blood, because the ocean erupted into a maelstrom of twisting bodies and huge snapping jaws as the wounded sharks were in turn attacked.

"This diverted attention from us and we were slowly moving our circle away from the sharks when the other boat appeared. They had been searching, but unable to see us in the wind and waves. When the great fins appeared, Hatch gave up all hope for our survival. He was about to head for shore when the fireball burst through the shark. As the other sharks churned the water to froth, the fireball drifted across the sea until it was directly above us. In the light, Hatch spotted our heads and came to the rescue. When the boat arrived, the brilliant light disappeared."

CHAPTER 52
Northward

Two months later, three men emerged from the trees to stand on a bluff overlooking a great valley. Huge mountain ranges on either side gave way grudgingly to vast forested slopes, sweeping down to meet each other in a sea of black timber covered with snow. Through the timber snaked a band of white, twisting and turning up the valley northward until it disappeared from sight. The scale of the scene was so enormous that the white path seemed but a few yards wide; in reality it measured more than a hundred yards across. It was bitterly cold, but Qimmiq's face, enclosed in a fur-trimmed hood, was flushed with excitement as he turned toward his companions.

"There is our road," he said, pointing down at the valley, his good eye gleaming triumphantly. All were dressed in heavy parkas, pants and mittens, and wearing snowshoes. In front of them were two wooden sleds piled with gear, each pulled by eight large dogs.

Tukor checked his body and for the hundredth time marveled at how warm he was. The exercise helped of course because the Inuits set a steady pace each day and he was carrying a pack, but the cold was beyond anything he could have imagined. Sometimes at night tree branches would simply freeze and split apart with a loud "crack." Yet his clothing kept him more comfortable than he had thought possible.

Even before the whale hunt, father and son had been busy bringing timber from the forest: splitting, shaping, and hardening the wood to fashion the two light sleds. Following the hunt, after a period of mourning had passed for the three lost men, the two had sought out the most skilled seamstresses and worked with them to create special clothing they would need for the far north. The New Mexican was focused on Talon's recovery and paid little attention to their activity. When two older women appeared and requested he stand for measurements, he obliged them, but it was several days before he asked his friends what it was all about.

"We're going home," said Tikaani. "You will need special clothes for the journey. That is," he added, "if you still want to come."

"Of course I want to come," snorted Tukor. "But winter is almost here. The boats are hull-up on the beach and the walls of the longhouses closed against the wind. Hatch and the men are talking about an elk hunt before the snow gets deep."

"Precisely," grinned the Inuit mysteriously. "It's the perfect time to go! Beside which, Shadow needs a new adventure to stop him from following you around like a puppy." It was true. The big wolf had bolted from Tikaanis's side, midway through the afternoon of the hunt, to sit on the shore of the bay and howl mournfully at the sky. The sound was so eerie that the whole village had gone quiet, suspecting that something terrible had happened. Hour after hour it went on, until Hatch's dugout appeared in the channel and the wolf saw Tukor. Since then the man could hardly turn around without stumbling over the animal.

Days went by in a blur of preparations. When the sleds were finished there were harnesses to make and dogs to be chosen. The Inuits were excellent judges of the animals they needed for the journey and picked 16 strong dogs from among the village pack. But when the time came to trade for them, Hatch and the men wanted nothing.

"Your friend was responsible for saving seven men from this village," said the leader. "A little more than two dogs for each life does not begin to cover our debt."

The night before departure the entire village gathered in Hatch's longhouse for a great feast. All the hearths down the building shared in cooking elk, salmon, and crab, with side-dishes of nut butter, dried huckleberries and crabapples, kelp and dandelion greens and cattail flatbread. The Makah people spared no part of their bountiful food sources with their new friends. When everyone had eaten their fill, they all gathered at Hatch's hearth to hear stories about their visitor from the south. Children told of his struggles learning to swim; someone related his competition for the mirror at the camp of the white men, but the most popular was the tale of the whale hunt, described by the two men who had witnessed what happened. Each telling was met with hushed silence.

Finally, Talon stepped into the light of Hatch's fire. A massive scar, stretching from his jaw halfway around his head, was still an angry red but there was a grin on his face. Tukor rose to meet him and the assembled people grew quiet.

"You saved my life," said the harpooner. "I would have drowned, or the sharks would have gotten me. Probably both." He held out a small pouch of soft leather. "I know the silver never leaves your neck, but perhaps this small gift can join it in memory of our friendship."

There was dead silence as Tukor opened the pouch and drew out a beautifully carved ivory whale three inches long. It was cleverly attached to a leather strap and when he slipped it over his head, the whale rested on his chest just above the medallion. Turning to face the gathered villagers, the New Mexican was met with thunderous shouts of approval.

Now, as he stood looking out over the vast panorama before them Tukor could feel the whale against his skin. His musings were interrupted by Tikaani.

"That is the reason we travel in the winter," said the Inuit, pointing at the white ribbon below them, Qimmiq and his dogsled already headed toward it. "The frozen rivers will take us to the northern sea before spring." With that he grabbed the leads, called to the dogs, and set out after his father.

"What about it, are you ready for another adventure?" inquired Tukor, staring at the great black head looking up at him. A red tongue lolled out in a wolfish grin and Shadow leaped forward to chase the disappearing dogsleds.

The Heirs of the Medallion
Ricardo
Book 5

SEVEN-YEAR-OLD RICARDO is spellbound by stories of the Arctic told to him by his great grandfather Tukor, now nearly blind from those adventures. When the creeks in the canyons dry up and the family is forced to move, Ricardo receives the medallion from Tukor. As he transitions into the modern world, it helps him face attempts on his life.

Years later, events take a dramatic turn for Great Grandfather, Juan and Sophia, when a strange stone fragment is discovered deep in the Andes mountains.